SLEEPING DOGS LIE

E.J. COCHRANE

Bella
BOOKS

2016

Bella Books, Inc.
P.O. Box 10543
Tallahassee, FL 32302

Printed in the United States of America on acid-free paper.

First Bella Books Edition 2016

Editor: Shelly Rafferty
Cover Designer: Sandy Knowles

ISBN: 978-1-59493-507-7

About the Author

In addition to teaching college English, E.J. Cochrane has had just about every job imaginable, including running her own dog walking company. When she's not writing, teaching, walking dogs or distracting herself with yet another employment adventure, she's one of those awful people who enjoys running (and somewhere in her closet has the dusty collection of marathon finisher medals to prove it). She and her partner live in Chicago with their three cats and their dog.

Dedication

For Jennie and Heidi. Like me, this book wouldn't be much without you.

Acknowledgments

Shortly after I started my dog walking business, two of my sisters asked me to join them for drinks to discuss *their* idea for a book that *I* should write. Since I love my sisters and beer almost equally, I agreed. I really didn't expect to start writing that book on my train ride home from the bar, but I couldn't help it. I loved their idea and the characters we created too much to wait, and I have had more fun writing this book than anything else I have ever written. So thank you Heidi Krystofiak and Jennie Tyderek for giving me this gift. Further thanks to Heidi, who in her role as Professional Nag effortlessly combined a menacing attention to deadlines and a compassionate understanding of my sometimes hectic schedule, and to Jennie for handling all of the computer issues that baffle me while not making me feel foolish for being baffled by them. Additional thanks to Amy Henry for sharing her expertise and answering all of my questions, even the silly ones. Also, since my attitude toward food is a lot like a five year old's, I am indebted to Patrick Doyle for helping me feed my characters something other than apples and desserts. Amy Cook, Kathy Rowe, Diane Piña and Lynda Fitzgerald—thank you for being the best team of beta readers a wimp like me could ever ask for. Your gently constructive comments have made this a better book. I am without proper words to express my gratitude for my partner, Sue Hawks, without whose unending support I never would have finished. Finally, thank you to everyone at Bella for doing all of the hard work and letting me play with words.

CHAPTER ONE

Matilda Smithwick stood in the lone patch of shade that fell on the sidewalk, though it made no difference. The record heat wave—now in its fifth day—had left her wilted two days earlier. Heat enveloped her, pulsating from the pavement, and the light summer breeze that stirred the leaves of the trees merely pushed the hot, humid air against her skin. Everything felt sticky, and she wanted to jump into Lake Michigan or at least find an air-conditioned building.

Goliath, the Great Dane standing immobile at the end of the six-foot leash Matilda held, didn't seem to notice the oppressive heat. He'd been sniffing a brownish patch of grass for at least five minutes and showed no signs of shifting his focus any time soon. Matilda wondered just how fragrant dead grass could be.

"Come Goliath," Matilda urged with a gentle tug on the leash, but as usual, Goliath ignored her. Obedience was a concept so totally foreign to him that Matilda wondered how he'd ever become a champion show dog. If Howard hadn't shown her the humongous silver cup Goliath had won, if he hadn't made her hold and admire it, she never would have believed that Goliath was a champion.

Certainly, he had the appearance of a champion. Like most Great Danes, he was massive—at one hundred twenty-five pounds he outweighed Matilda, and his shoulder came up to her hip. Granted, her hip was only about three feet off the ground, but his size relative to hers made him seem all the larger. He had a regal bearing as well. In his deep brown eyes, Matilda could almost see several centuries of his breed's history. By far, though, his most impressive feature was a thick, steel-colored coat. Goliath's owner, Howard Monk, had proudly told her that Goliath was a perfect blue, the term for that color in the breeding and showing worlds. In the bright midday sun, Goliath's sleek fur shone like a fresh coat of enamel paint.

Still, it took more than beauty to be a champion. Even Matilda, with her limited knowledge of and interest in dog shows, understood that. So how had wispy, frail-seeming Howard Monk commanded show-winning behavior from a dog who apparently didn't even understand the basic command "sit"? Maybe Goliath just didn't listen to women.

After an eternity of sniffing, Goliath discharged roughly two drops of urine on the intriguing patch of grass. Then he trotted to Matilda and butted her hand with his head, apparently requiring praise for his efforts.

"Good boy," Matilda obliged. "Finally," she muttered. They'd been outside for ten minutes, and this was the first business Goliath had tended to. She had no illusions that her time with Goliath would be easy, but it would certainly be lucrative.

Having recently fallen down his basement stairs, Howard, with a broken arm and fractured femur, would be wheelchair-bound for at least a month. (Matilda thought that a very optimistic diagnostic estimate—Howard looked like a giant wound.) He'd offered Matilda twenty dollars per walk, three walks a day, every day until he recovered. She'd quickly done the math and decided that Howard's money would be a great boon to her business, Little Guys Pet Care, a small but steadily growing dog walking company on Chicago's North Side. Now that she knew what she was in for with Goliath, though, she thought she'd use some of the money to buy herself a hard-earned treat. Maybe some new running shoes.

A few feet ahead of Matilda, Goliath released a torrent of urine on a single, drooping dandelion. He'd obviously found the perfect place to relieve himself, and Matilda hoped that meant he'd find complete relief before they returned to his home. Stunned, she watched as Goliath plopped down in a curbside garden and began rolling and wiggling his massive body, flinging dirt and clumps of greenery about the area and ruining some unfortunate gardener's flower bed. *He's never going to poop*, she thought, as she used treats to lure him from his floral playground.

At the end of the alley behind Goliath's house, he finally took care of the rest of his business, waited only ten seconds for Matilda to clean it up, then bounded, in all defiance of the heat, to his yard. The rickety gate proved no challenge for a dog Goliath's size, and Matilda doubted it would even hold a toddler back. Once in the yard, Goliath made his way to the back door.

In the short time Matilda had been walking Goliath, he'd always made it inside the house before her. Howard ordinarily parked his wheelchair at the kitchen door, keeping watch from inside, and as Goliath barreled through the yard, Howard would open the back door with the carved ebony walking stick he'd used before his accident. By the time Matilda entered the mercifully cool kitchen, Goliath would be devouring a bone that, by its appearance, came from a brontosaurus.

Today, though, Goliath sat on the deck whining and pawing pathetically at the door.

"What's wrong, buddy? Did your dad forget?"

Goliath whimpered and hit the door with his giant paw once more.

"Maybe he fell asleep," she offered as she reached for the door handle. Goliath ignored her and dashed inside, presumably for his dinosaur bone, but he barely glanced at it as he ran in search of Howard. The clamor of Goliath's footfalls on the hardwood floor filled the air and apparently drowned out the sound of her voice as she called out for her client. "Howard? Mr. Monk?"

She followed the sound of Goliath in search of Howard from room to room, down the long hallway, past the bathroom and the stairs to the basement (the ones Howard had fallen down just a few days earlier), then through the dining room. She continued to yell his name as she moved through his house, and the longer she went without seeing or hearing Howard, the more time slowed, as if she was entering the slow-motion lead-up to a car crash.

In the living room, she stopped. Goliath's long, low, sorrowful moan penetrated the mental and emotional miasma that had enveloped her since she entered the house, and she realized she had no idea how long Goliath had been crying.

"Howard?" she squeaked. Her voice, timid and childlike, seemed to come from somewhere outside of her, as if someone else had spoken in her voice.

On the floor in front of the fireplace, Howard lay in a thick, dark pool. His empty wheelchair sat behind him, just outside the widening ring of blood. Beside him lay his walking stick and Goliath's dog show trophy, which looked like it had fallen from the mantel. Howard's head was twisted to the side, and his unblinking eye seemed fixed upon Matilda. She saw a deep gash on the back of his head from which blood still flowed, and she knew without question that Howard Monk was dead.

CHAPTER TWO

Matilda sat at the top of the stairs to Howard's front porch. Despite the great heat, her teeth chattered, and her body shivered uncontrollably. Someone, perhaps the officer who had escorted her outside and parked her on the porch, had covered her trembling shoulders with a fusty woolen blanket, but she had no memory of this happening. At her feet, Goliath lay whimpering and occasionally howling since the police had managed to coax the poor animal away from his owner's body. He had blood on his front paws and nose. Matilda debated about wiping it off—her stomach churned at the thought of touching Howard's blood, and the part of her brain that still functioned wondered if that would be considered evidence tampering. But when she heard Goliath's moaning sigh, her heart broke for the poor creature. Overcoming her own revulsion, she reached down and wiped the blood away with a corner of the blanket, which she then dropped to the ground away from her and Goliath, and resumed her shivering.

Around them, uniformed police officers moved cautiously about the scene, but Matilda barely registered their presence. She couldn't seem to focus, and when she closed her eyes all she saw was poor Howard sprawled out in his own blood. She felt that she'd stood above him, frozen, for hours, but it must have been only a few moments before the police had arrived. How they'd known about Howard's death, Matilda couldn't say. Her first call, as always in times of crisis, had been to her best friend, Gwendolyn.

Matilda had grown up in the same part of the city as Gwendolyn, but they hadn't met until they worked together as lifeguards in high school. During their first summer at work, they'd formed a friendship that thrived even after the beaches closed. Over the years, challenges at school, family drama and issues with dating (and marriages for Gwendolyn) had solidified their bond. Their closeness was such that, although Gwendolyn detested being called by a nickname (and had even divorced her second husband in part because he called her Gwen), Matilda got away with calling her Dottie.

When Matilda had decided to start Little Guys, Dottie had helped her get the company off the ground, even wrangling clients from her circle of rich, dog-loving friends. In fact, it was Dottie who had introduced Matilda to Howard, so it had seemed like the most natural thing in the world for Matilda, when she'd been confronted with the harsh reality of Howard's dead body, to call her best friend. She'd actually been on the phone with Dottie, asking her friend what to do, when the first uniformed officer arrived. Startled, Matilda had hung up on Dottie (an offense she'd pay for later), but after that she wasn't sure what had happened. She tried to sort out her confusion, but instead of clarity, she thought only about the disturbing scene by the fireplace: Howard, his empty wheelchair, his blood, Goliath's dog show trophy and the walking stick which, she realized with a start, must have been used to beat Howard to death. Matilda's stomach revolted again.

"Excuse me!" Gwendolyn's unusually sharp voice penetrated Matilda's thoughts. "Officer Hernandez, is it? I assure you that I have no intention of compromising your precious crime scene. At this very moment, I can think of at least a hundred venues more appealing to me than the site of a murder investigation. Be that as it may, that wretched creature, that despondent wreck of a human being seated over there has called me to her aid, and I will not abandon her in her hour of need. Now, let me pass."

Immobile and stunned, Officer Hernandez sputtered something about his superior officer.

"Dear boy, I would worry less about that and more about what the Superintendent will have to say after I speak with him. He just hates it when I'm unhappy," Gwendolyn added with the pouty expression that had almost always gotten her whatever she wanted. Officer Hernandez shifted uncomfortably before Gwendolyn played her next card. "Of course, my close friend the mayor, who, incidentally, has tried everything to return to my good graces since he missed my fundraiser last month, might also be interested in your efforts to prevent me from providing much needed solace to that sad little girl withering on the porch."

Gwendolyn smiled sweetly then strode elegantly past the flustered and dumbfounded Officer Hernandez and up the walkway to Matilda. From her Lanvin handbag, Dottie extracted a lacy handkerchief and spread it on the porch before seating herself beside Matilda. Shaking his head and muttering, Officer Hernandez attempted to turn his attention back to securing the crime scene, but for a few moments he simply stood at the edge of the sidewalk, mouth agape, looking cowed and a bit shell-shocked from his encounter with Gwendolyn Hunter.

Matilda understood his dumbfounded response to Dottie's imposing presence. She'd seen it repeatedly. Even without the stylish but not even remotely comfortable-looking heels that she preferred, Dottie was taller than the average male and stunning, with strawberry blond hair, luminous hazel eyes, full lips and remarkable breasts—a gift from her first husband and the means by which she had met her second. Add to that her rich and occasionally breathy voice, and Dottie's paralyzing effect on most men was a given.

On the porch, Dottie draped her arm around Matilda's shoulders and drew her old friend close. "Maddie, sweetheart, what *have* you gotten yourself into?"

"Poor, poor Howard," Maddie said.

The two women sat in silence until Maddie's shivering subsided. "Have you contacted your second in command to let him know what's happened?" Dottie asked.

Maddie's head snapped up. "I can't believe I didn't even think of that. Oh, God. I don't know how long I'll be here. Someone needs to cover my walks. What if no one's available, Dottie?"

"Not to worry, kitten. I'll take care of everything."

Undoubtedly grateful to remove her designer-clad body from Howard's dusty porch, Dottie grabbed Maddie's cell phone, glided in the direction of the still apprehensive Officer Hernandez and began clearing Maddie's schedule.

"Patrick, doll, it's Gwendolyn Hunter. How *are* you?" As Dottie's voice trailed off, Maddie felt a momentary relief. Dottie and Patrick would make sure that all of Little Guys' business was tended to. The police would find Howard's killer. Somehow everything would work out.

Her peace of mind ended abruptly, however, when a gravelly male voice pronounced—or rather, mispronounced—her name. Like everyone, he read it phonetically rather than smashing the middle three letters together in a "D" sound.

"It's 'Smiddick,'" she offered before looking up into the face of the most perfect representation of a haggard detective she'd ever seen. His craggy face was a patchwork of wrinkles. What hair he had was short and gray, and his physique, stoop-shouldered and thick in the middle, indicated that life and work had worn down a once fit body.

"I'm Detective Fitzwilliam. I need to speak with you."

CHAPTER THREE

After asking innumerable questions and issuing a warning about not leaving town, Fitzwilliam sent the two friends on their way. Maddie's relief at being dismissed lasted only until she looked at Goliath. Still whimpering, he sat trembling beside the police officer who held his leash. The thought of abandoning him with strangers filled her with sadness, but looking at the stern faces of law enforcement milling about made her doubt that she could violate some police procedure or other and ask to take Goliath with her. She sincerely hoped that someone from Howard's family or one of his friends had a safe, loving home to share with Goliath.

Even though Maddie lived just a few blocks from Howard's house, and even though Dottie, under normal circumstances, refused to ride in Maddie's Jeep (citing her lifelong disinterest in taking an urban safari), Dottie insisted on driving her friend home. "You are in no condition to drive," she declared and plucked the keys to the Wrangler from Maddie's hand before Maddie could protest.

In under five minutes, Dottie pulled into the garage behind Maddie's home—a two-flat greystone that Maddie had, through incredible luck, purchased as a foreclosure. Mr. Smithwick, who had spent summers in college working construction and now owned his own contracting company, had helped Maddie fix the place up in the three years since she bought it. At times she'd doubted that they would stop finding problems that demanded their immediate attention so that they could finally make the place livable. As soon as they'd revived the ancient plumbing, the roof had sprung a leak. Then there were the terrifying electrical issues. By the time they'd started refinishing the floors, they had done so much to bring the building back from the dead that she had begun referring to her house as Lazarus, but by then, she and her father were determined to see the repairs through to the end. In time, they transformed old Lazarus into a beautiful, comfortable home. Father and daughter still saw a few areas for improvement (Maddie dreamed of someday replacing the original and considerably drafty windows), and they tackled various projects as free time and surplus income presented themselves. Last year Maddie had taken on a renter on the second floor to help pay for the improvements she and her father had yet to undertake.

"Sit," Dottie commanded as she propelled Maddie into the living room. "I will take care of everything. Just relax and recover from your ordeal." Dottie stooped to remove her friend's shoes.

"I'm not sick, Dottie." Maddie sighed and allowed her feet to be hoisted, less than delicately, onto the couch.

"Nonsense." Dottie fluttered her hand in the air, as if swatting an insect. "We have been best friends for eons, and at your darkest hour, you called me to your aid. There must be something that you need from me. So tell me what I can do for you, buttercup, and then consider it done."

Maddie sighed once more, knowing that it would be easier to make her friend feel useful than to convince her that she needed to provide nothing other than companionship. There would be no peace until Dottie had a task. "Since you ask, I'm sure Bart needs some relief. You can just let him go in the yard to do his business."

"Say no more." Dottie rose, strode to the back door and called to Maddie's rescued mutt. "Bart, angel, Aunt Dottie is here to save you from your overburdened bladder." From beneath his shaggy gray eyebrows, Bart threw a bemused glance Maddie's way before trotting out the door.

Dottie stayed in the kitchen, presumably to wait for Bart to finish up, but as Maddie settled more comfortably into her appointed recovery station on the couch, she heard what sounded like the start of cocktail hour. At ten forty-two a.m. Glad to have something other than Howard's death to focus on, Maddie listened as Dottie moved about the kitchen, opening and closing cabinet doors. She heard the musical tinkle of ice cubes hitting glass, the squeaky thunk of a stopper leaving a bottle and the delightful sound of some form of alcohol moving from bottle to glass. Then the back door opened again, and in a moment, Bart and Dottie both entered the living room.

"Drink." Dottie thrust a tumbler of amber liquid in Maddie's face. "And don't argue."

"Who's arguing? I think, unconsciously, this might be the reason I called you and not my mother," Maddie answered before taking a grateful swallow of bourbon. "She would have made me chamomile tea."

"Not that I don't appreciate a compliment—backhanded or otherwise—and not to downplay my own powerful presence, but perhaps Maureen Smithwick, Legal Eagle, might have been the wiser choice under these circumstances."

"How so? I hate chamomile tea."

"Precious," Dottie huffed as she pulled Maddie forward to jam a throw pillow behind her back, "you're a suspect."

"What are you talking about? As usual, you're overreacting."

"I? Overreact? You wound me."

"Gwendolyn," Maddie grumbled in exasperation. She knew what was coming next, knew that nothing ever stopped Dottie when she decided she had to be protective, yet Maddie tried to deter her friend from acting on her behalf.

"Don't 'Gwendolyn' me. That...officer," she uttered the word as if its foul taste sat on her tongue, "grilled you for an eternity—"

"Or forty-five minutes in Normal People Land."

"He practically took your mug shot there on the veranda."

"Veranda?" Maddie muttered. "Never mind. He was just doing his job, Dottie. He questioned me as a witness, nothing more. Even if you're right, he's sure to figure out that I wouldn't kill anyone. Don't give the poor man a hard time."

"His job, sugar pie, is to find Howard's assassin, not to harass my friends."

"Fine. You're absolutely right. But if you distract him by butting in, it will just take him longer to eliminate me as a suspect. Please, Dottie, just let it go."

Dottie folded her arms across her full chest and exhaled loudly and emphatically. "You may have a point. But if his plebian mind prevents him from seeing your innocence for long, I will not remain silent."

"Thank you." Maddie swallowed the remainder of her drink. "Now, will you please just sit with me?" she asked. "After you get us another round."

"I'll be back posthaste."

Prompted by Dottie's overactive imagination, Maddie's mind wandered back to her experience with Detective Fitzwilliam. She'd thought his questions totally innocuous at the time, but were they? Questions about her affiliation with the victim (a term that chilled her) and about her movements during the time of the murder took on an ominous tone in her mind. At the time her biggest fear was that she hadn't been very helpful—her working relationship with Howard had been so short that she didn't know much about him. She didn't even know what he did for a living.

Her favorite question—"Are you in the habit of calling your friend rather than the police in emergencies?"—had seemed merely in keeping with the detective's gruff, sarcastic personality. Looking back, it seemed much more damning. Even her answer (that she had panicked and thought Dottie would know how to handle the situation) sounded incriminating now.

When Dottie returned with their beverages, Maddie slowly sipped her second drink, actually taking the time to enjoy the flavor of the bourbon as Dottie chattered about things normally uninteresting to Maddie. Today, they seemed fascinating. In the middle of an amusing anecdote about an ice sculpture at some vapid high society gathering, Maddie's cell phone rang.

"It's probably Patrick checking in," she offered to Dottie as she grabbed the phone from the coffee table and glanced at the screen. "No, it's my mother."

"Good God! She knows!" Dottie's exclamation was met with a strenuous eye roll from Maddie.

"Hi Mom," Maddie answered then fell silent. As she listened to her mother, her face grew more ashen, her expression more concerned, until, finally, she hung up the phone.

"Are the police coming to arrest you?" Dottie, who could apparently no longer contain herself, exclaimed.

"No," Maddie answered dolefully. "Granny's in the hospital. She collapsed this morning. The doctors are running tests. They don't know what's wrong."

"Oh honey," Dottie answered as she folded Maddie in a firm embrace. "This is just not your day."

CHAPTER FOUR

"I despise hospitals," Dottie proclaimed as she and Maddie searched for the elevators that would take them to Granny Doyle's room.

"Nobody likes them, Dottie," Maddie replied curtly.

"Not true," Dottie countered as she swept around a corner with a certainty disproportionate to her knowledge of the hospital's layout. "Matthew always said that he loved them."

"Well, he is a doctor," Maddie answered before grabbing Dottie's arm to guide her in the opposite direction. "I guess that makes sense."

"He said he liked the smell."

"What?" Maddie stopped at what she hoped were the right elevators and repeatedly pressed the call button. "Who would enjoy the smell of hospitals? It's all bodily functions, antiseptics and institutional food. As odors go, that's just...gross."

"There is a reason he's my ex, lamb chop," Dottie replied as the car arrived and she stepped inside.

With a soft shushing sound, the doors closed out the harsh light and noise of the hospital lobby, leaving Maddie with nothing to distract her from her overactive imagination. She turned to Dottie, who was checking her hair and makeup in the reflective surface of the doors. "What if she's dying?" she asked.

Dottie tapped Maddie's shoulder in an awkward but well-intentioned way. "What did your mother tell you was the matter when she called?"

"She didn't. Just that Granny had been admitted and the doctors were running tests."

"Sounds ominous," Dottie offered dryly. "You have yet to see her and haven't a clue why she's here," Dottie added when Maddie's expression failed to register anything other than terror. "It may be a bit premature to start planning her funeral."

"Dottie, she's seventy-six years old. At her age, everything is potentially deadly."

"All you know is that she's in the hospital. You might give the old girl a chance before you prop her up at death's door."

"What if she has cancer?" Maddie asked, seeming not to have heard a word her friend had said.

"What if she ate bad sushi?" Dottie countered.

Maddie's glare spoke volumes, but Dottie ignored her. "She could be feeling the aftermath of an ill-advised culinary adventure, and now she's weak and dehydrated, a desiccated husk clinging to the beacon of modern medicine's restorative powers."

"Are you even capable of being serious?" Maddie asked before exiting the elevator and heading down the corridor.

"Do you think she'll have one of those fluid humps they give to cats?" Dottie smiled sweetly as they approached the room.

"I'm done talking to you. Let's just go in."

The first thing Maddie saw when she walked through the door was her mother, who smiled wanly at her. Put together as always in a designer suit, only slightly rumpled by the heat of the day and the stress of Granny's ordeal, Mrs. Smithwick seemed calm, but her disheveled red hair and puffy eyes indicated how worried she was. Maddie hugged her mom, grateful for both her presence and her composure. In addition to the rest of the trials of the day, a hysterical Maureen Smithwick would have been more than Maddie could handle.

"Can the living pin cushion get a hug?"

Granny, fettered to the bed by an impressive array of tubes, cords and wires, looked more irritated than ill. She almost never got sick, not even with a cold. She said she had too much to do to be bothered with illness. Maddie hugged Granny as best she could with all of her hardware, and instantly recalled the only other time she'd ever known her grandmother to be under the weather. That had been one of the scariest moments of Maddie's childhood.

Maddie had practically grown up at Granny Doyle's house. Both of her parents were working tirelessly to establish their careers and spent little time at home. Considering how often they were both gone, it was a wonder they had managed to produce three daughters, but Maddie adored Granny Doyle, who showered June, Harriet and Maddie with so much love that Maddie didn't mind her parents' absences much. Granny cherished the time spent with Maddie and her sisters and usually found something fun or educational for the sisters to do, so the girls loved being with her.

When Maddie was seven, Grandpa Doyle had died suddenly. He'd gone to work one morning feeling fine, but before lunch he'd had a heart attack at his desk. The whole family had been shocked by his unexpected passing, and Granny in particular was disconsolate over the loss. She ate little and slept less. Maddie watched in despair as a shell of her grandmother shuffled disinterestedly through her days. Something had to revitalize Granny, so Maddie called upon her older sisters to help her intervene.

That summer, a little more than a month after Granny had lost her best friend and begun to fade, Maddie, Harriet and June had dragged their grandmother to the beach in an effort to cheer her up. Granny had always found the lake beautiful and often brought the girls there to appreciate it with her. Surely a relaxing day in one of her favorite spots would lift Granny's spirits. The day was hot—in the mid-nineties with little cloud cover—and after a couple of hours of watching the girls swim and build sand castles, Granny grew listless. She doled out the peanut butter and jelly sandwiches that the girls had packed and gave each of her granddaughters a juice box, telling them that she would eat later. She herself had a headache and felt a little nauseous. Grabbing her grandmother's arm to try to lure her into the water, Maddie felt how hot and dry Granny's skin was. Her breathing was funny too. Something was definitely not right. Just before Granny passed out, June asked, "What's wrong, Granny?"

In a flurry, others around them had rushed to Granny's aid. One of the lifeguards, a young blond girl, had moved Granny into the lake while they all waited for the ambulance to arrive. Her quick action to help cool Granny Doyle may have saved her life. It certainly curtailed the harsher symptoms of the heat stroke that had caught Granny and her granddaughters so off guard.

Maddie had felt guilty about the incident for weeks, long after Granny was out of the hospital and on her way to a full recovery. If not for her stupid and futile plan to make Granny happy again, she never would have gotten so sick. When Maddie had finally worked up the courage to apologize to her grandmother for making her ill, Granny Doyle dismissed her concerns. "Nonsense," she'd said and then explained in her direct way that she reckoned she wasn't ready to join Maddie's grandfather just yet, and she was grateful for the warning. Then she'd given Maddie a cookie and sent her on her way. That had been the end of it.

"So Dottie," asked Granny Doyle, the only person on Earth besides Maddie who was allowed to call Gwendolyn anything other than Gwendolyn. "How are you? Any marriage prospects?" She smiled at her granddaughter's oldest friend.

"I am woefully single at present."

"Well, get cracking, girl. I get too few opportunities to put on my dancing shoes, and we know my granddaughter isn't in any rush to walk down the aisle."

"Granny," Maddie interjected, "until very recently it wasn't legal for me to get married."

"Well, dating wasn't outlawed for you, was it?"

Dottie's laugh sounded like a whip crack in the quiet hospital room.

Granny stared sternly at her now silent granddaughter. "Have you gone on a single date in the last two years?"

Maddie hated talking about her failed relationships, especially with Granny, who wholeheartedly believed that Maddie's exes were always entirely at fault, simply because they just weren't good enough for Maddie. Granny refused to see that few women were knocking themselves out to woo a short, freckled, small-breasted dog walker. Rather than get into a dissection of her love life with Granny Doyle and her all-too-eager stooge, Dottie, Maddie threw her jaw out as an answer.

"I didn't think so. You don't need to spend any more time moping over someone who up and left at the first sign of difficulty. You're a young woman, practically a child. Go out. Kick up your heels and have fun. The way things are going with you, I'm likely to get married before you do," Granny added when Maddie remained mulishly silent. "Dottie, you're my only hope."

"I'll consider it my mission, Mrs. Doyle."

"I've told you a thousand times, Dottie. Call me 'Granny,' like everyone else does."

"And you'll have to tell me a thousand more times, Mrs. Doyle. Now, what's going on with you? We rushed over here, and we must have answers."

"A whole lot of fuss is what's going on." Granny Doyle fluttered her hand in the air as if to brush off the seriousness of the situation. "I've seen more doctors in the last two hours than I've seen in my entire life, and not one of 'em knows a damn thing. At this rate it'll be Christmas before I go home."

"Mother," Mrs. Smithwick cut in. "You passed out. They need to find out what happened and how to fix it before they can send you home."

"Nonsense," Granny spat. "It was a little dizzy spell. No call for all this commotion."

"You fainted? Did you fall? Were you hurt? Was anyone with you?" Maddie hugged her grandmother again.

"You're as big a worrywart as your mother. The only thing wrong with me is that I'm stuck in this bed."

"Her neighbor was over for coffee," Mrs. Smithwick interjected. "Thankfully they were sitting on the couch when your grandmother had her 'dizzy spell.' Mrs. Harkin called the ambulance right away, and then she called me."

"Been a while since you visited, Matilda," Granny said, pointedly changing the subject.

"Granny, it's been a week."

"Well, in old lady years that equals a month."

"Since when are you an old lady?" Maddie asked.

"Since you stopped visiting," Dottie answered to Granny Doyle's delighted approval.

"Your mother's too frazzled for a conversation. She keeps wanting to talk about my health, and since I'm too stubborn to admit when something's wrong, according to some folks, it's been a rather one-sided discussion." Mrs. Smithwick shook her head tiredly and sighed. "So tell me what's going on with you."

"I've just been working a lot. Nothing worth talking about."

Dottie snorted and, in response to Maddie's warning glare, tried to cover with a cough.

"Sounds like you disagree, Dottie. What secrets is my granddaughter keeping?"

"Just that she's wanted for murder." Dottie deliberately ignored Maddie's piercing scowl.

"What?" Grandmother and mother asked simultaneously and swung their heads in Maddie's direction.

"As is usually the case when Gwendolyn speaks, that is an extreme exaggeration." Maddie explained what had happened with Howard and the police that morning, being certain to stress that she had not been arrested or accused of any crimes. Nor had she been in any danger

"This sounds serious. What are you going to do?" asked Granny, who was obviously relieved that someone else was the object of concern.

"I'm going to carry on with my life and let the police do their job."

"And what if they start looking at you as a suspect? Dottie thinks they already are."

"I didn't kill Howard, Granny. I'll be fine."

"Matilda, your reputation is everything. It has to be unimpeachable."

Maddie had heard this line from Granny Doyle all her life. Whenever Maddie had misbehaved in any way, Granny Doyle had set her right not with punishment, but with a succinct explanation of the importance of her honor and her good name.

"You can't very well print 'Entrepreneur and Suspected Murderer' on a business card." Dottie smirked, earning another icy glare from Maddie. "Shouldn't you be more proactive?"

"And do what, Granny?"

"Prove that you're innocent!"

"How? By finding the real killer? I'm a dog walker, Granny, not a detective, and this isn't an episode of *Murder, She Wrote*."

Granny Doyle huffed in resigned exasperation, and Dottie turned to Maddie's mother. "Can you do anything to help, Mrs. Smithwick?"

"I don't see how, Gwendolyn. Maddie hasn't been charged with anything, and even if she had been, I'm not a defense attorney."

"Details, details." Dottie, who not half an hour before had been so rational, now abandoned reality entirely. She waved Mrs. Smithwick's all too logical remark aside with a fluttering of her fingers. "Can't you just brush up? Read a few books and, *voila*! You're Perry Mason!"

"Gee, Dottie, I think my mother neglected to renew her Magically-Transform-into-a-Fictional-Attorney license this year."

"Honestly, I don't know how you can be so glib about your future."

Maddie refrained from pointing out that none of Dottie's current flight of fancy had anything to do with her future. Dottie's expanding imagination would just steamroll over any pleas for common sense, fact or even sanity. "You could end up in prison, cupcake, and you would look awful in one of those orange jumpsuits."

"First, no one looks good in a prison jumpsuit. They're not designed for Fashion Week, Dottie. Second, it doesn't matter," Maddie added through clenched teeth, "because I am innocent."

Dottie huffed dramatically, and Granny Doyle shifted everyone's focus. "What about that poor dog? Goliath, is it? What's going to happen to him?"

"That's what you're concerned about, Mom?" Mrs. Smithwick looked even more worn down than she had when her daughter arrived.

"Maddie is as stubborn as her old Granny. If she thinks she can trust the police to clear her good name and save her reputation before the next ice age, who am I to convince her otherwise? But that dog needs someone he knows, someone he can rely on. Is there anyone for him now that his master is dead?"

Maddie didn't know, and her heart sank at the realization that she hadn't done more to protect Goliath earlier. Some dog lover she was.

Back home a short while later, Maddie gave Bart a giant hug. "Granny's right," she told him. "I have to make sure Goliath is okay." She also couldn't easily dismiss her grandmother's surprise over her own acceptance of the situation. Granny Doyle obviously thought that Maddie should be more proactive, less of a doormat, and the more she considered her grandmother's tenuous health, the less Maddie liked the idea of her innocence in any way seeming ambiguous.

After letting Bart outside, she pulled out the card that Detective Fitzwilliam had given her earlier in the day. He'd told her to call if she thought of anything. Maddie knew that he meant anything useful for solving the case, but she didn't know where else to start. And maybe he'd give her some ideas about proving her innocence, inadvertently of course.

The phone rang once before the detective answered in his gruff voice.

"Fitzwilliam."

"Hi, Detective. This is Maddie Smithwick. We met this morning." What a stupid thing to say. The man was a homicide detective, not a potential suitor.

"Miss Smithwick." He said her name in the same wrong way he had earlier, even though she'd twice now pronounced it for him correctly. Somehow, though, she didn't feel this was the appropriate time to stress the proper pronunciation. And it was entirely possible that he mispronounced it intentionally, just to exasperate her. "I've been meaning to call you."

"Oh? Is there news in the case already?" She thought she sounded suspicious and immediately cursed Dottie for planting that seed.

"No, just a couple of questions I need to ask."

"Shoot." She'd just said "shoot" to a cop. What was wrong with her?

"In the time that you'd been walking Mr. Monk's dog, had you established a routine schedule?"

"Mostly. There was some flexibility, but I tried to be consistent for Goliath."

"So you walked him about the same time every morning?"

"Yes. Howard asked me to be there close to eight. That was no problem since I don't usually have early morning appointments."

"So it's likely that people in the neighborhood knew your schedule," Fitzwilliam stated plainly. "And you said that you walked him for twenty-five minutes?"

"That was the goal. Goliath didn't make it easy, though."

"Meaning?"

"Sometimes he'd dally and wouldn't, um, do his business until we'd been out for over twenty minutes, so we'd stay out longer. Other times he was done in under ten minutes and wanted to head right back home. I would have to coax him into a longer walk."

"I see." The detective paused in his questioning, but not long enough for Maddie to ask her own question. "Do you know anything about the trophy?"

Did he mean the monstrous silver cup Goliath had won? That was the only trophy that Maddie could remember seeing. "It came from a dog show. I don't remember which one. Is that important?"

Fitzwilliam ignored her question and continued. "Did you ever handle the trophy, Miss Smithwick?"

She ground her teeth at his repeated destruction of her name. Was it really so difficult to say "Smiddick"? "A few times, actually. When we first met, Howard made me take it off the mantel so he could properly boast about his champion show dog." Maddie recalled how Howard had praised Goliath's color, his bearing, his regal presence, while the object of his acclaim had lain on the floor slobbering over a bone, completely oblivious to Howard's raving tribute. She had become instantly fond of both of them. "Once or twice after that we went through the same routine. Howard was so proud of Goliath."

"He's a good-looking dog. Reminds me of my old dog," Fitzwilliam offered, showing the first indication of humanity. "It's a shame what happened to the poor guy."

What did he mean? Poor Goliath? Now she was really worried. "What happened?"

Detective Fitzwilliam hesitated briefly before explaining that Howard's ex-wife, Shelly—his next of kin and only family— had no interest in taking Goliath. "He's at Animal Care and Control."

"That's terrible. Do you know—can I get him?" Maddie couldn't help her plaintive tone.

Again Fitzwilliam hesitated. When he answered, some of the gruff edge was missing from his voice. "I think that would be fine," he said.

CHAPTER FIVE

For Maddie most days started with a run. Logging three to five miles first thing in the morning helped her to clear her mind, ponder her schedule and get energized for the day ahead. After a run, she always felt healthy, cleansed and renewed. She had tried to explain the feeling to Dottie, but her friend couldn't comprehend intentionally courting perspiration. Dottie preferred swimming, where sweat went unnoticed.

Sometimes Maddie brought Bart along. He enjoyed the activity, and she enjoyed his company, even though the run usually got derailed by squirrel chasing or stick chewing. However, she'd thought better of bringing him in the oppressive heat. It was one thing to inflict torture on herself, quite another to force an animal to take a brisk dash through the outdoor equivalent of a sauna. Truth be told, she benefitted more from her time alone. At least, that's what the fit of her jeans told her.

Today, however, a run was completely out of the question. Her pounding head reminded her of the turmoil in her life. Between Howard's death, Granny's health, Fitzwilliam's questions and

Dottie's bartending, she was bound to be hurting. Any one of those conditions could induce a migraine, but combined, they added up to circumstances that called for the clarity that comes from running but a symptom that prevented it entirely. Plus, Goliath standing beside her bed, resting his chin on her pillow and issuing a pathetic, whimpering sigh, reminded her that she now had two dogs to care for.

She had sprung Goliath from Animal Care and Control near closing time the previous day, having delayed her rescue because the mere thought of the pound depressed her. Like many Chicagoans, Maddie thought of Animal Care and Control as a dumping ground for the city's unwanted or troublesome animal population, and her past dealings with city employees led her to believe that the department would be staffed by a dour and disagreeable group that seemed burdened by employment. When she arrived, though, she was met by workers and volunteers who challenged her perception. Despite the usual sadness Maddie always felt in animal shelters, here she also sensed an air of gratification. These workers didn't always witness happy endings, but clearly there were enough to sustain them.

Maddie selected a young man from among the employees and prepared to embark on the lie she had rehearsed to secure Goliath's release. She was Howard's niece, she would say, there to rescue his beloved dog and the one piece of her uncle that could soothe her grieving soul. But as soon as Maddie described Goliath, the young man's face lit up.

"You must be Miss Smithwick!" he exclaimed. "We heard you might come by."

Based on the mispronunciation of her name, she presumed that the tip had come from Detective Fitzwilliam. Despite her continued irritation with him, Maddie was beginning to appreciate his apparent love for animals. In short order she had filled out all of the necessary paperwork and walked out the door with Goliath, whose dejected shuffle to the car gave her hope that she was doing the right thing. A loving home, even if temporary, had to be better than shelter life.

Bart, who now slept on the other side of the bed, snoring quietly with his tongue hanging out, had taken to Goliath right away. Maddie had worried about the stress of introducing the dogs and had asked Dottie to help her, but as soon as Goliath had entered the house, Bart had sniffed the larger dog's hindquarters, wagged his tail and then had gone to his toy box and grabbed his second favorite squeaky toy—a pink polka-dotted pig whose tail unfurled as it squealed—which he dropped at Goliath's feet. Goliath had squeaked the toy once with his giant paw, then nudged it with his nose before retreating to the corner to curl up on the floor. Dottie interpreted the scene as a release from her dog-chaperoning duties and began mixing drinks, an activity at which she excelled.

This morning, groaning as she sat up, Maddie put her hands to her throbbing temples momentarily then dragged herself to the kitchen to start her day. For several minutes she stood paralyzed by her inability to decide if she should take some ibuprofen first or if it would be better to start making coffee and then deal with her headache. The coffee pot was closer to her, so she started there.

"I'm doomed," she moaned as she stooped to pick up the dogs' food bowls and a wave of nausea and dizziness hit her.

The kibble she'd given Goliath remained untouched. He hadn't even sniffed at it when she'd offered it to him. She didn't know if he was too depressed to eat, or if his tastes were too refined to settle for the food Maddie had offered him. She figured emotional stress was the more likely cause, but just to be sure, she offered the dogs wet food for breakfast. Bart appeared as soon as the can opened, and he happily gobbled up his helping. Goliath still refused to eat, but he sat beside Bart and followed him outside once Bart finished his meal. At least Goliath had a friend, Maddie thought. She would figure the food issue out soon. Not that she didn't have a thousand other equally pressing issues weighing on her mind right now.

After a slow and painful start to her morning, Maddie made her way to the small storefront just a few blocks from her home where Little Guys was based. The heat hadn't abated yet, and she was glad to step inside the air-conditioned building. Patrick had left a detailed note for her, the gist of which was that everything had run smoothly without her and that he hoped she was feeling better after her ordeal. She smiled, in spite of recent calamities, and thanked whatever bit of luck had brought him to her door two years earlier.

One of the first people she had hired, Patrick had started working with her as a way to earn extra cash while in college. He'd quickly shown himself to be responsible, reliable and intelligent, and she'd relied on him heavily as the company expanded. Together with his obvious love for animals, Patrick was the natural choice for a promotion to manager when the company had grown large enough to require one. Since then, he had also taken over the marketing. She didn't know exactly how he did it, but business was booming and had been for months. Recently, he'd begun suggesting additional services that they might offer, and Maddie loved the direction her little company was taking.

Once she finished reviewing Patrick's notes from the day before and checked her schedule for the day, she called her grandmother.

Granny answered the phone after two rings, sounding hoarse and a little confused, which did nothing to lessen Maddie's worries about her grandmother. But once she realized it was Maddie, Granny's voice regained its naturally warm and alert qualities.

"I was wondering how long it would take you to check up on me. Both of your sisters have already called, and your mother just showed up." Granny sounded almost jovial now. "I'm more popular than a condom salesman outside a whorehouse."

Ignoring her grandmother's immodest commentary, Maddie asked if there had been any developments since yesterday.

"Not that I've heard. It's all tests and no answers. I think these doctors are running tests just to see how many tests they can run. They've stuck me for blood so many times I have more holes than a colander."

"How do you feel?"

"Like a lab rat. I'm ready to go home where at least I'd be comfortable while I wait for scientific confirmation that I'm fine."

Granny spoke a little more about her disappointment in the doctors, and Maddie felt reassured, thanks to the irritated speech, that her grandmother was essentially her usual, healthy, assertive self. Perhaps Granny was right and she really was fine.

"And have you stayed out of trouble since yesterday?" Granny asked, interrupting Maddie's thoughts.

"I have. No one else has turned up dead, and I have a houseguest." Maddie explained about rescuing Goliath from the pound. "I'm going to take care of him until I can find him a permanent home."

"Good girl," Granny replied enthusiastically, and Maddie was happy to have pleased her grandmother.

"He's still adjusting, but I think he's better off."

"I'm sure of it," Granny said. "You're a wonder with animals."

"Thanks Granny," Maddie beamed and then indicated that she had to end their call and return to work.

"Your timing couldn't be better," Granny muttered. "The vampires just returned for what little blood they haven't already taken." Before hanging up, Granny had ordered Maddie not to let her old grandmother rot away in the hospital without visiting.

Relieved that her grandmother sounded better, Maddie shifted her focus back to business. She liked to greet her employees, touch base with them and make sure they looked presentable before they went walking through the neighborhoods with her company's name and logo on their chests. Before seeing her small fleet of walkers off that morning, she still had to review the log of all the walks from the previous day—a task with which she normally concluded her day—but yesterday had been no ordinary day. Once the business had taken off, Maddie had instituted the walk log, initially on paper and later in its electronic iteration. The system helped Maddie keep track of her walkers, produce client invoices and verify the payroll. She loved the simplicity of it (now that the bugs had been worked out), and her clients loved receiving text or email updates on what their dogs were up to while they worked.

She had barely started the program when her cell phone rang. It was her mother.

"Hi Mom," Maddie answered brightly. "I'd ask how Granny is, but she just told me."

"That's actually why I'm calling, sweetie." Maddie felt her smile disappear. "I heard what your grandmother told you and, well, you know your Granny."

Maddie's good mood plummeted. She *did* know her Granny, and she should have known better than to adopt optimism wholesale based on Granny's word alone. "Let me guess. She's doing no better, but she's putting on a brave face and protecting everyone from the truth."

"You're mostly right," Mrs. Smithwick answered gently. "Last night her vital signs got worse. The doctors put her on IV fluids, and there's been some improvement."

"I see."

"We're still waiting for answers, though."

"Is she going to be okay, Mom?"

"I wish I knew, Maddie. I wish I knew."

After ending the call, Maddie turned away from her computer, unable to concentrate on her work, however important it was. She reflected instead on her conversation with her grandmother. Obviously Granny was concerned about the mess with Howard's death, but that was stress that she just didn't need. She was glad that she hadn't mentioned her plan to start looking into Howard's death to her mother or her grandmother, and she didn't intend to let either of them know, at least not yet.

She herself didn't know exactly where to go next. There were so many angles to consider. It was possible that an intruder had killed Howard. If so, Maddie had no hope of finding the murderer in a city of almost three million people. On the other hand, it didn't seem likely that, in the short span of time she was gone with Goliath, someone had randomly wandered in off the street and beaten Howard to death. What was the motive? On top of that, Howard would have had to let the killer in, an unlikely scenario and an almost impossible task for a man in his condition. It seemed more likely that the murderer was someone Howard knew and, if so, Maddie needed to find out who knew Howard.

Glancing at the clock to be sure it wasn't too early to rouse her diva friend, Maddie pulled out her cell phone and called Dottie.

"Morning dove," Dottie cooed into the phone, apparently unfazed by the nuclear cocktails she'd whipped up the night before.

Aggravated by her friend's effortless composure, Maddie dispensed with pleasantries. "I need a favor, Dottie."

"Was another of your clients slain? Do you need bail?"

"You're loving this entirely too much," Maddie grumbled.

"On the contrary, precious, I am overwrought with worry."

"Thanks," Maddie offered wryly.

"What can I do for you?"

"Do you know Howard's ex-wife Shelly?"

"I've had the pleasure of her company on more than one occasion." Dottie's tone oozed disapproval. Shelly must not be up to Gwendolyn's standards.

"Will you visit her with me?"

"Why?" In that one syllable, Dottie expertly blended curiosity and contempt.

"Her ex-husband was just brutally murdered. I thought I might offer my condolences," Maddie explained as if it was obvious. She hesitated before sheepishly adding, "And ask a few questions about Goliath and Howard."

"A-ha!" Dottie whooped. "You're snooping, aren't you?"

"Fine, yes, I'm snooping."

"Shouldn't you leave this to the police?"

"Weren't you just yesterday insinuating that the police are incompetent and I'd be doomed if I left matters in their hands?"

"Let's not exaggerate, kitten."

If not for needing a favor, Maddie would have pointed out how ludicrous that statement was, especially from Dottie.

"I never said it would take forever, but honestly, it could take them years."

"And do you really want my innocence, my integrity, to be in question for that long?"

"Of course not, but you're talking about trying to find someone who beat an old man to death, someone who might still have been in the house, lurking in a dark corner, ready to pounce when you walked in. Did you consider that?"

"No." She actually hadn't thought of that possibility. She'd been too shocked in the moment to consider much of anything beyond the corpse splayed on the floor in front of her. That image haunted her, popping into her head almost every time she closed her eyes. It was another reason she didn't want to sit idly by while Howard's murder became just another cold case for the Chicago Police. Maybe if she searched for answers, if she did something other than wringing her hands and waiting for time to pass, maybe then her mind would quit tormenting her. Maybe the twinges of guilt she felt (irrational though it was) would subside.

"You'd be safer dressing like a quail and going hunting with Dick Cheney," Dottie chastised her further.

"I promise I won't do anything remotely brave. I just want answers to a few questions.

"Will you help me or not?"

"Fine." Dottie sighed her answer more than she spoke it. "I will schedule a meeting with Shelly and call you back within the hour."

Wondering if she was really prepared for what she was getting herself into, Maddie returned to her computer and the work that awaited her.

CHAPTER SIX

Just before four o'clock that afternoon, Dottie parked in front of the building in Uptown where Shelly Monk lived. Nervous and enjoying the air-conditioned comfort of Dottie's Mercedes, Maddie stayed rooted to the passenger seat and surveyed the area. Shelly's building, one of those brick courtyard complexes ubiquitous in the city, looked run-down and neglected, yet sturdy. Newspapers and advertisement circulars, some still in their plastic bags, had piled up on most of the doorsteps, and the grass, which was overgrown and at least fifty percent dandelions, was festooned with scraps of paper, flattened cups and plastic grocery bags that stirred in the light breeze. Maddie wondered if anyone other than Shelly actually lived there.

"It's not exactly Lake Point Tower, is it?"

"It reminds me of my youth," Dottie shuddered. She usually avoided talking about where and how she had grown up, preferring to live in the much more luxurious now. "Are you sure you want to do this, kitten?"

"Not really," Maddie answered, finally getting out of the car. "But we're here, so we might as well go in. Are you ready?"

"As I'll ever be." Dottie locked her car and strolled up the walkway.

The conditions inside Shelly's third-floor apartment thankfully did not reflect the sad state of the building's exterior. The space was tidy and simple, with basic IKEA furnishings and dozens of plants. Instead of an air conditioner, Shelly had a couple of oscillating fans that pushed the hot, humid air around the room. And Shelly herself was, well, a surprise. Based on her encounters with Howard, Maddie had expected to meet a sweet, older woman, delicate in build and demure in nature, but the woman before her contrasted completely with Maddie's expectations. Shelly was large—not fat—but tall and solidly built. She had a wide, flat face, which seemed to hold a permanent frown, and her straw-colored hair had been permed into a cotton candy-like frizz on top of her head. Maddie could not picture Howard married to this woman.

In all fairness, though, when Maddie had met Howard, she had thought he was gay, so she had a hard time picturing him married to any woman. Of course, Maddie knew of plenty of gay men and lesbians who had succumbed to family or social pressures and entered into heterosexual marriages. Too late, they realized that they couldn't deny their true selves, and the marriages had ended, often bitterly. Perhaps that was what had happened to Shelly Monk.

"Thank you for seeing us on such short notice, Shelly," Maddie offered sincerely.

"I've only got a couple hours between shifts," Shelly grumbled, her voice like a rasp. She motioned to the couch for them to sit and then sat in the armchair opposite them. "Make it quick, okay?"

Shelly's brusque manner put Maddie on edge. She felt awkward offering this disinterested woman her condolences, but that was what they had come for. "I'm so sorry about Howard's death. I know you weren't married anymore, but still, it's such a shock. Howard was a wonderful man. You must feel awful."

Shelly snorted and reached over to pet a sleek, white cat that had curled up beside her. "You must not have known him long."

"Just a couple of weeks actually." Maddie smiled, reflecting—as she'd done so often lately—on her first meeting with Howard.

"It shows. Most people who knew Howard well wanted to kill him."

Struck dumb by Shelly's blunt commentary, Maddie simply stared, but Dottie spoke up. "Yours must have been a whirlwind romance then." Dottie flashed a saccharine smile at Shelly. "Or did you willingly marry someone you loathed?"

"I guess you know a thing or two about marrying the wrong man, don't you, Gwen?" Shelly sneered.

Dottie's eyes flashed with anger and she shifted in her seat, gathering herself for a fight, but Maddie laid a calming hand on her friend's arm before Gwendolyn's seething anger fully unleashed itself. She wanted Shelly amenable and talkative, not combative or defensive.

"Why would you say that people who knew him wanted to kill him?" Maddie asked, trying to sound innocently curious.

"Because it's the truth." At Maddie's startled expression, Shelly huffed, "I was married to him for fifteen years. Trust me, he was a bastard."

"It seems you bring out the best in people," Dottie taunted.

Shelly glared at Dottie, ready to pounce, but Maddie jumped in as referee once more. "I'm sorry, Shelly, but I'm having a hard time reconciling the Howard I knew with the man you're describing. I just can't imagine what he did that was so terrible."

"Let's just say, when Howard wanted something, Howard got it, no matter what anyone else wanted."

"That's surprising. Howard was so generous to me."

"I'm sure," Shelly snorted after looking Maddie up and down and making no effort to conceal her assessment. "Howard was generous to me, too, when I was young and pretty."

Shocked, Maddie didn't know if she was more bothered by Shelly's thinly veiled allegation or by the fact that the only woman to call her pretty in the last two years was a bitter harridan accusing Maddie of sleeping with her most likely gay ex-husband. Before she could address Shelly's incorrect assumption about her relationship with Howard, Shelly had launched into a story. "We used to live in Colorado. Beautiful state, not like this flat hell. Not long into our marriage, when we were still in love, Howard helped me start my own business, a garden center. I loved getting my hands dirty, working the soil." Shelly looked almost joyful as she lost herself in her memory. "I worked all the time, twelve hours a day or more, just to get the place on its feet. I didn't see Howard much, but he said he didn't mind. He liked to see me happy."

"He sounds positively malicious," Dottie hissed.

With another glare at Dottie, Shelly resumed her tale. "After a few years the business was doing great. I was thinking of opening a second location. I really thought Howard would go for the idea. It was a great investment. Instead he ruined everything."

"What did he do?"

"I came home from work one day to a For Sale sign on the lawn. Howard had decided we were moving to Chicago. He never asked if I wanted to leave or what I thought about it and wouldn't listen to my side at all. He just sold our place, hired movers and brought us here. I couldn't restart my business in this horrible place, so now I'm working even longer days at two crappy jobs just to make ends meet."

"Why didn't you just stay in Colorado if you loved it so much?" Dottie asked.

"Wish I would've, but Howard invested the money to start my business. Technically it belonged to him. He sold it out from under me, so I had no home and no job."

"How upsetting for you." Maddie spoke conspiratorially.

"I was furious. Could've killed him." Shelly seemed oblivious to the incriminating nature of her comments. "And I was still mad at him about that damn dog."

"You mean Goliath?"

"I wanted a cat, but Howard just went out and got himself a puppy."

"Who doesn't love a puppy?" Shelly's scornful expression answered Maddie's question clearly.

"After that it was all about that damn dog. Practically every word out of Howard's mouth was about the dog's perfect color, or his coat, or his temperament. All I could see was a slobbering mess that pooped all over my floors, but Howard was obsessed. If he wasn't fussing over the dog, he was doing research on it—reading books on Great Danes and going online."

"He knew nothing about the breed before he got Goliath?" Dottie sounded surprised.

"He knew nothing about dogs! He woke up one morning determined to get one, so he found a breeder on the Internet. By dinner time we had our own hairy poop factory."

"Wait. The breeder wasn't bothered by your...reservations about dogs?"

"I never met him. I went to work, and Howard drove nearly halfway across the state, paid the man and drove back home with a puppy and enough supplies to fill half a pet store. Most of it he didn't need. He had no idea what he was doing, but he said that's what the Internet was for. I guess the breeder gave him some websites to look up."

"The breeder didn't provide information to Howard himself?" Dottie's disbelief increased. "He just gave him a purebred dog and sent him on an Internet expedition?"

"As far as I know, that's what happened. After that, all of Howard's time and money went to the damn dog, and I was left out in the cold. Howard even cooked for that dog. Can you imagine?" Shelly huffed.

"Really? Do you happen to know what he cooked?" Maddie asked brightly.

Shelly scowled at her with such hostility that Maddie shrank into herself.

"It's just that I've taken Goliath in for the time being, and with everything that's happened recently, he's not eating. I thought maybe if I gave him what Howard did, he might start eating again."

"I don't care if you feed him ground glass," Shelly snarled. "That damn dog ruined my marriage." Maddie thought it highly unlikely that Goliath, rather than Shelly's unpleasant disposition, was the cause of her union's demise, but she refrained from saying so. "I have to get ready for work. I think you better leave now." Shelly spat the words at them as she stood to let them out.

"Of course." Dottie rose gracefully and dragged Maddie to her feet. "We appreciate your…hospitality."

Back at the car, Dottie hesitated a moment before getting in. She asked, "What's your take, Sherlock? Is Shelly our killer?"

Maddie pulled her damp T-shirt from her skin and waited for Dottie to unlock the car. The humidity had increased, raising Maddie's hopes that a thunderstorm would cool the city by nightfall. "I wouldn't put murder past her," she answered and got in the car. "That is one angry woman."

"In my experience with her, that was one of Shelly's good days."

Maddie shook her head in wonder. How had Howard stayed married to Shelly for fifteen years? "But why would she wait so long? Why not kill him before they left Colorado when he first made her so angry? Or even while they were still married? Why wait until after the divorce? It doesn't make sense."

"Shelly isn't the embodiment of sensibility and rational thought, sugar."

"I believe that, but if she works as much as she claims, would she really have time one morning to swing by her ex-husband's house and bump him off while the dog walker was out with Goliath?"

"It doesn't seem likely." Dottie pouted as she drove back north. "Damn. I was really hoping she did it."

When Dottie turned down Maddie's street, Maddie asked her to drop her off at Little Guys instead. "I've got some work I need to catch up on."

"There's no time for work, peaches. We have to get you ready."

"Ready for what, Dottie?" she asked warily.

"I've arranged for a special covert snooping party. We'll crack the case wide open!"

"I suddenly have a very bad feeling about all of this."

CHAPTER SEVEN

"Well, that was a bust," Maddie grumbled to the dogs as they accompanied her down the hall from the kitchen to her bedroom. Following Shelly's unintended advice, Maddie had tried cooking for Goliath, but he had barely nibbled at the chicken she'd prepared for him before turning away. Bart had taken care of the remainder of the food, so he was in high spirits, but she was beginning to worry about Goliath. She would try again with steak, but if he refused to eat even that, then a trip to the vet would be in order.

Upon entering her bedroom, Maddie found Dottie in a full swoon over the contents of her wardrobe. Maddie's closet doors were thrown open, her drawers divested of their effects, and most of her clothes were strewn across the bed. Dottie stood over the pile muttering, "Nothing. There's absolutely nothing." Hesitantly and with great scorn, she lifted a pair of Maddie's shorts from a heap of similar garments. "Really, Maddie, not even the Crocodile Hunter owned this many pairs of cargo shorts."

"They're for work, Dottie." Maddie snatched the offensive attire from Dottie and began refolding her clothes to put them away. "I have a lot to carry when I walk dogs, and cargo shorts hold everything I need perfectly."

"Please stop saying 'cargo shorts.' Just the sound of the words is giving me hives." Maddie rolled her eyes. "I suppose you have a perfectly logical explanation for these." Dottie gestured at a large mound of T-shirts heaped on the opposite end of Maddie's bed.

"They're comfortable."

"Matilda Elise Smithwick. Fashion is *not* about comfort. It is how we announce ourselves to the world." Maddie braced herself for whatever disparaging comments Dottie was about to make regarding her wardrobe. "Honestly, you work so hard at staying fit. You should be parading about in your underwear. Well, not *your* underwear. I've seen that." Maddie glowered at her friend. "But you drape your body in baggy, formless, *cotton* attire. How is any young woman going to fall for you if she can't see you?"

Doubting the magnetic powers of her physique, Maddie chose to ignore that aspect of Dottie's commentary. "Do you really think I'm the only lesbian who wears cargo shorts and T-shirts?" Maddie smirked at Dottie's obvious disdain and changed the subject. "Can you fill me in on the agenda for tonight?"

"As you know, I have many associates in the dog show community."

Maddie nodded. She did know of (but failed to understand) Dottie's obsession with dog shows, and though she balked at calling a collection of purebred elitists a community, her best friend was among them. For that matter, some of Maddie's top clients had come from Dottie's connections to the world of dog shows, so Maddie kept her judgment to herself.

"I lead a small group of owners. We meet regularly to socialize and to discuss rules and regulations, breeding practices—all very important matters."

"Of course." Maddie tried to keep the sarcastic edge from her voice.

"Sometimes we gather to watch televised AKC events."

Growing bored and impatient, Maddie broke in, "Before you start drooling over the results of the Westminster Dog Show, what does this have to do with me, Howard's death or your plans for the evening?"

"I do not drool, Liebchen." Maddie merely stared at Dottie and waited for an answer to her question.

"Since you asked—indelicately, I might add—until yesterday, Howard was a member of our group. Following the untimely demise of one of our own, I have called the surviving members of our little group together for an intimate soiree in Howard's honor."

"And I'll be there why?"

"So that you can talk to those who knew Howard best in order to sniff out clues."

"You're taking me to a cocktail party so I can spy on Howard's friends?"

"Essentially," Dottie answered, slightly miffed that her elegant evening and brilliant plan had been reduced to such a coarse interpretation.

"And you want me to look more like a dog snob, less like a dog walker," Maddie said, filling in the conspicuous blank in Dottie's statements.

"We aren't snobs. We simply understand the significance of good breeding." Maddie didn't really see the distinction. "But yes, you do need to look the part, and regrettably, we do not have time to shop."

"In that case," Maddie grinned smugly, "you might check the closet in the guest bedroom. I think you'll find something more suitable there."

Maddie hadn't finished her sentence before Dottie vanished from the room, rousing the dogs, who trotted after her. "Praise Dior!" Maddie heard her friend exclaim from the room down the hall where Maddie kept the clothes she wore infrequently: dresses, business suits, off-season items. The extra closet space was at least one advantage of being perennially single.

Momentarily Dottie and her canine retinue returned with three options—all dresses.

"I'm so proud of you, little one. You may choose one of these." Maddie reached for her favorite of the three, and Dottie instantly rejected Maddie's choice—an emerald green sheath that complemented her green eyes. "No, not that one. This is the one." She thrust a black, sleeveless cocktail dress at Maddie. "And do something about your hair. A ponytail will not suffice!"

By eight p.m. Maddie had made the rounds of Dottie's Lincoln Park condo and mingled with several of the amassed dog show mourners, most of whom seemed to have known or cared about Howard only peripherally. Though he was the night's honoree, few people offered more than innocuous, superficial commentary about him. As Maddie feared, they mostly wanted to talk about their dogs.

She had met Melissa Spalding, owner of a Beagle saddled with the optimistic name Champ. "That's his call name," Melissa explained before rattling off a litany of words that comprised Champ's official dog show name. Assuming she'd never have reason to address Champ by his other name, Maddie promptly forgot it and tried to focus on Melissa, a difficult task as her bland coloring and doughy features made her seem washed out. She habitually pushed her wire-rimmed glasses up with the side of her hand, and in the rare moments when she wasn't talking about Champ, Melissa pursed her plump lips as if ruminating about which wondrous Champ factoid to roll out next.

Taking advantage of one such break in the ode to Champ, Maddie asked, "How well did you know Howard?"

"Oh, we hardly ever talked. Howard was a Great Dane and I'm a Beagle, so we really didn't have much in common."

"Different worlds really," Maddie offered dryly and searched for a way to escape before Melissa launched into another Champ devotional. Exasperated and lacking Dottie's social poise and finesse, Maddie gave up. "Excuse me, but I have to... go," Maddie said and then left Melissa to find another ear into which to sing Champ's praises.

She had a similar experience with Hoyt Bailey, a reedy, balding man whose cairn terrier, Henry, was allegedly related to Terry, the dog who'd played Toto in *The Wizard of Oz*. Maddie learned all about Henry's diet, his grooming rituals, his weight (in pounds and kilograms) and, of course, his lineage. The one thing she didn't learn was Hoyt's connection to Howard. Hoyt simply refused to be sidetracked into talking about anything other than his dog.

After her fourth such encounter, Maddie began to think that Dottie's special spying mission was a flop and that she was in way over her head. If she couldn't even figure out a way to get these people to talk about Howard instead of their dogs, then what hope did she have of figuring out which clues to follow? If they even had any clues to offer. Disappointed by the decreasing likelihood of finding Howard's killer in this crowd or elsewhere, Maddie retreated to the corner occupied by Anastasia, Dottie's pampered Russian wolfhound—Borzoi, she corrected herself. In this crowd, Anastasia was a Borzoi. Proper terminology notwithstanding, Anastasia was a sweetheart, and lying there forlornly on her plush dog bed, she seemed in desperate need of snuggles.

Squatting in the most ladylike fashion allowed by her dress (and still likely to induce an apoplectic fit in Dottie), Maddie began petting Anastasia. She was just getting going on a mini dog massage, eliciting a satisfied grunt from her dog companion, when a man's voice behind her startled her.

"Dog lover or just antisocial?"

Maddie stood and turned to see a handsome, sandy-haired man smiling at her. Dottie had pointed him out earlier when he had arrived with his partner, but Maddie hadn't had the chance to speak to either of them yet. She couldn't remember their names.

"Both actually." Maddie smiled then introduced herself.

"Adam Whelan." He shook Maddie's hand, and her memory clicked. His partner, Albert Silver, was in commercial real estate. "My partner is much better at these things than I am." Adam pointed to a slightly older, equally handsome man who didn't seem at all bothered by the unfortunate fact that he was on the receiving end of Melissa Spalding's Champ chatter.

"I know what you mean," Maddie offered. "I'd prefer being at home with my dog and a good book."

"What kind of dog do you have?" Adam perked up, and Maddie realized the mistake she'd just made.

"He's a mutt I rescued from a shelter."

Adam Whelan's eyebrows shot up in surprise. "A mutt? Be careful who you say that to in this crowd."

"It's not really the fan club for mixed breeds, is it?"

"If you're a mutt lover, how did you end up socializing with the dog show set?"

"I love all dogs, but Gwendolyn is my best friend, and I was Howard's dog walker. I wanted a chance to meet his friends and bid him farewell." Adam seemed to flinch at the mention of Howard, so Maddie pressed further. "Did you know Howard well?"

"A little too well," Adam answered acidly.

"It doesn't sound like you were friends."

"We weren't." Adam didn't mince words. "I'm hardly surprised that he was murdered."

Finally, she had encountered someone who could help her advance her investigation. Maddie didn't know whether to be thrilled at her first break or horrified at being face-to-face with someone who disliked Howard, maybe enough to want him dead.

"Then why are you here?" she asked, trying to sound more curious than accusatory.

"Albert," Adam offered, as if that explained everything.

"He was friends with Howard?"

"God, no. Albert couldn't stand the conniving weasel."

"Then...?"

"Albert loves Gwendolyn, would do anything for her. She said it was important for the whole group to be together, so here we are."

"I see," Maddie said, not sure that she saw anything.

"And it's not like we'd be running into Howard, is it?" Adam chuckled at his own macabre joke, then deftly changed the subject before a stunned Maddie could ask more about his relationship with Howard. "You said you're a dog walker? Do you have a card? We're looking for someone new for our poodle, Alphonse."

Maddie produced a business card from the purse Dottie had forced her to carry and resisted commenting on the abundance of A-names in the Silver-Whelan family (why offend a potential new client—or possible killer?) while Adam launched into the Alphonse variation on the purebred praise she'd been subjected to far too much of already. In the middle of a sermon about proper grooming, Adam spied someone bustling through the front door.

"What's *she* doing here? Ruth hated Howard more than Albert and I did."

Glancing in the spot where Adam's gaze was directed, Maddie saw Ruth Charles, the one member of the group that Dottie hadn't expected to show up and the last to arrive. She stood in the foyer, surveying the small crowd gathered in Dottie's living room. Maddie found her oddly compelling, in a train wreck sort of way.

Artificially blond and average in height and weight, Ruth Charles carried herself with a poise and bearing not unlike Dottie's, though Ruth's toad-like face held more haughty superiority. Much more. She was dressed well, elegantly even. Maddie didn't know designer clothes (in spite of Dottie's persistent nudging "in the right direction"), but she could tell that this woman did. She was as well put together as Dottie, yet there was a striking contrast between the two women. Where Dottie's clothes seemed natural to her, like an extension of her being, an expression of her character, Ruth Charles' attire seemed out of place on her, like she was wearing a costume. Maddie wanted to know just what those clothes were designed to hide.

Excusing herself from Adam's company, she made her way to Ruth Charles and introduced herself.

Ruth limply took Maddie's outstretched hand. "You don't belong here," she said. "Or are you new?"

"I'm Gwendolyn's friend," Maddie explained as Ruth flicked her eyes over Maddie with unrepentant derision. Maddie already loathed her.

"Do you even own a dog?"

"As a matter of fact, I currently have two dogs."

Ruth seemed slightly more interested now. "What breed?"

"One is a Great Dane."

Ruth's eyebrow arched in surprise. "Really? My Duchess is a Great Dane. What breeder did you use?"

"Actually I sort of inherited him—Howard's dog, Goliath. I took him in after—well, you know." Maddie simply couldn't discuss Howard's death as baldly as Adam Whelan did. "I'm keeping him for the time being. Just until I can find him a good home."

"That dog is a menace," Ruth hissed. "He should be destroyed. Just like his owner."

Maddie guessed that asking for advice about the breed was out of the question.

"What about your other dog? What breed is it?"

"*He*," Maddie stressed the pronoun, hoping to convey to this woman that her dog was more than a possession, so much more than an *it*, "is a mutt I rescued from a shelter."

"A mutt? Are you deranged? What would compel anyone to have a mutt? They're useless, inferior creatures."

Maddie was an inch from throttling Ruth Charles, who either didn't know or didn't care just how offensive she was.

"I would never have a dog of questionable origins. Purebreds are the only dogs worth owning. They're predictable in temperament, in appearance—"

"In disease," Maddie cut in. She saw no reason to feign politeness with this crone. "So much swimming in such a tiny gene pool means that purebred dogs are at a higher risk for cancer, tumors, hip dysplasia, heart disease and neurological diseases." Maddie checked each condition off on her fingers as she ran through the list.

"What could you possibly know about the matter?" Like most people with an opinion, Ruth wasn't prepared to let hers go.

"Quite a bit, actually. Dogs are my business—"

"In a janitorial capacity. You're just a dog walker. That's hardly the same as a veterinary degree or breeding experience."

"I know enough to understand the stress and suffering purebreds endure just to fit a ludicrous, manufactured aesthetic." People around them were beginning to stare, mostly at Maddie and her radical opinion of purebreds, but Maddie didn't care.

"That ludicrous aesthetic, as you call it, is a necessary tool for gauging a dog's caliber, though it isn't a foolproof method. Even some who appear to have good breeding—" Ruth Charles scrutinized Maddie once more. "Well, looks can be deceiving."

"Are we still discussing dogs?" Maddie asked. She was ready to pounce when she saw Dottie bearing down on them.

"Matilda, dear, come with me. I have someone I'd like you to meet." She grabbed Maddie's arm to pull her away, then turned to her guest. "Can I get you anything, Ruth? A fresh glass of venom, maybe?"

Ruth huffed angrily but made no response before Dottie forcefully steered Maddie away from the scene she'd helped cause.

"What is wrong with you?" Dottie hissed in Maddie's ear.

"She started it," Maddie whined.

"She always does, cupcake, but now that you've outed yourself, so to speak, no one else is going to talk to you."

As the disappointing truth of Dottie's statement sunk in, Maddie's cell phone rang. She glanced at the screen, surprised by the call. "I better take this."

Gwendolyn's look told her that this was only a momentary reprieve from her much-deserved scolding, and Maddie slunk guiltily back toward the mostly empty foyer where Ruth Charles still stood, surveying the scene, probably searching for her next argument.

"Detective Fitzwilliam," Maddie answered. "What can I do for you?"

"Miss Smithwick," Fitzwilliam said, and Maddie gave up any hope of ever hearing him pronounce her name correctly. "I spoke with Shelly Monk this evening."

"Oh?" Maddie had no clue where this conversation was headed.

"She mentioned that you and your friend visited her today." Maddie still wasn't certain why Fitzwilliam was bringing this up. "She said that you asked a lot of questions about Howard and his dog."

"Well, we wanted to offer our condolences, and it seemed like a good opportunity to find out more about Goliath and how to care for him." Maddie hoped she sounded sweetly innocent. She certainly didn't feel that way.

"I see." Fitzwilliam seemed utterly unconvinced. "As long as it was just a social call and not you suffering from delusions of being some civilian super sleuth. I don't need any help with my investigation."

"I have no plans to interfere, Detective. I want the truth about Howard's murder to come out."

"Then let me do my job and you do yours."

Maddie muttered her assent before hanging up. She resisted the urge to stick her tongue out at Ruth Charles as she passed her on her way back to the party.

CHAPTER EIGHT

The next day, the first order of business for Maddie was a visit to her grandmother's hospital room. Given all of her investigative activity the day before, she hadn't had the opportunity to see Granny Doyle or even call her again after their early morning chat. She'd also again neglected her continuously increasing workload, but unlike Granny, that was in no danger of going away any time soon. Feeling a little guilty, she arrived at the hospital early to get more one-on-one time with Granny. Time alone with her grandmother was a rare treat, especially since her hospitalization, and she wanted Granny's input on her investigation so far.

Though Maddie had initially thought better of telling her grandmother that she was looking into Howard's death, she now felt that just telling Granny what she'd learned (though it wasn't much) and what she was thinking about all of it would provide her with a fresh outlook on the case and help her put things in perspective. But that didn't mean that Maddie wanted to let her mother in on her investigative activities. She wasn't sure which of Maureen Smithwick's characteristics—hand-wringing mother or reproachful attorney—would dominate the disapproval Maddie was certain she'd face, but she knew at least one side would emerge to let Maddie know she was making a mistake.

When Maddie entered Granny's hospital room, she found her grandmother scowling at her breakfast of cement-like oatmeal and dry toast. To Maddie's surprise, Granny looked no better for all the medical attention she had been receiving. Her coloring leaned more toward sallow than blooming, and her wavy hair, normally a stunning white since it had finished its transition from auburn a few years earlier, now hung in limp, oily, grayish tendrils around her shoulders. Maddie had hoped she would find relief in seeing her grandmother, but she felt herself growing more concerned instead. Still, she put on a brave smile and greeted her grandmother cheerfully.

As it turned out, Maddie needn't have bothered rushing in to beat the crowd. Granny had told Mrs. Smithwick, "I don't need a babysitter," and had forbidden her from showing her face in Granny's hospital room before noon. Granny said that Harriet and June planned on visiting in the evening, hopefully at Granny's house after her liberation from medical purgatory, so Maddie had plenty of alone time with her grandmother.

"These fool doctors haven't learned a lousy thing except for how much blood an old woman's veins can hold," Granny complained. "Incompetent, the whole lot of 'em. I hope the police are having better luck finding your client's killer. Any word on that?"

Maddie pounced on the opening Granny gave her and told her everything.

"So you've eliminated the ex-wife as a suspect, but you've added three people in her place," Granny said, processing Maddie's detailed account of her activities the day before.

"And I have no idea why they hated Howard. They weren't exactly forthcoming." As Dottie had predicted, no one had talked to Maddie after her encounter with Ruth Charles. The party had dissolved not long after, and a weary and frustrated Maddie had gone home, tended to her dogs and gone immediately to bed.

"What about Dottie?" Granny's brow was furrowed in her seriousness. "You say they're her friends. Maybe she knows what's got them so cross."

Maddie chuckled to herself. Who but Granny Doyle would refer to possible murderers as "cross"?

"She might, but she's a little cross herself."

"Because you and Cruella de Vil got into it at her party?" Maddie nodded. "Don't fret, child. Dottie loves you too much to stay mad at you for long. She'll let it pass soon enough."

"I hope so," Maddie said, not sounding the least bit hopeful. She'd apologized to Dottie last night, but knowing Dottie, she would have to offer something more extravagant than "I'm sorry" to smooth her ruffled feathers. Maddie wondered absently if this was an offense that called for flowers.

"She will," Granny declared with finality and smiled reassuringly at Maddie.

Maddie was relieved to see Granny so positive about something even though her mystery illness and extended hospitalization were taking an obvious toll on her physical and emotional well-being.

"How is Goliath taking to his new situation?" Granny asked, still seeming upbeat.

"I'm not sure. He loves Bart and the backyard—Howard didn't have a very big yard. But I don't think he's eaten since the…incident," Maddie offered. "I need to look up his file today and see if I can make an appointment with his vet."

"Well, I hope his doctor is more competent than the nincompoops they've got running this place. Seems like they just handed out white coats and stethoscopes to anybody who stood in line long enough to get them," Granny cast a severe glance at the young doctor who had entered her room, "regardless of whether they know how to do their blasted jobs." The young man had the good sense to look sheepishly away from Granny during her outburst.

"Speaking of people doing their jobs, I should probably go do mine." Maddie didn't really want to leave her grandmother, but she couldn't keep putting off her work. Before she left, she promised Granny that she'd call or visit again soon, and she offered the doctor a sympathetic glance as she passed him. Considering Granny's decreasing patience with medical professionals, he was in for a scolding, and Maddie thought she would spare him the embarrassment of watching as it unfolded.

At the office, she checked her schedule for the day, pleased to see that she and Patrick had an appointment to meet a new client—Pam Withers—at four o'clock that afternoon. She loved how her business continued to bloom and again considered Patrick's suggestions for growth. They'd discussed offering doggie day care services for pups who might need more activity and attention during the day. She had also contemplated expanding to include a grooming and dog spa facility. She'd started an informal search for local spaces large enough to accommodate a play area as well as a grooming and pampering station. She'd seen a couple of spots that met her criteria but wasn't sure she could manage the rent right now. At the very least, Maddie thought, she could run the numbers and dream a little.

Before getting completely swept up in visions of her own pet care empire, Maddie reminded herself of all of the tasks currently demanding her attention. The first order of business was contacting Goliath's vet. She hadn't yet transferred Howard and Goliath's information to her computer, so she searched through the paperwork from all of her new clients, mentally adding "update records" to her to-do list. Around the middle of the pile, she located the information sheet Howard had filled out just a few weeks earlier. At the bottom of the page where Maddie left space for any additional information that might be helpful in tending to the animals in her care, Howard had written, "Champion Show Dog!" She smiled wistfully at the shaky block letters then looked to the top of the form for the information she sought.

Maddie was surprised to learn that Goliath's vet, a Dr. Sheridan, was located just a few blocks from her house. While it certainly would have been convenient for Howard to visit a neighborhood business, she had expected him to opt for some chichi, overpriced Lincoln Park vet over a local doctor, given Howard's tendency toward extravagance where Goliath was concerned. She breathed a sigh of relief at the realization that she could walk Goliath to his appointment rather than spending up to an hour in traffic, and she was pleased at the opportunity to check out Dr. Sheridan's practice.

The office itself was a relatively new business to the area, just a couple of years old. Maddie remembered watching with curiosity as the space was renovated. In a short time, the construction crew had transformed the old dive bar (where Maddie had spent far more time and money than she should have in college) into a modern, state-of-the-art veterinary practice. Maddie passed it regularly as she walked around her neighborhood, glancing in the windows, still curious, but she would never leave her vet, a soft-spoken older woman who combined holistic and conventional medicine to keep her clients happy and healthy.

As Maddie reached for her phone to call Dr. Sheridan's office, her business line rang. At the other end of the line, a distraught woman informed her that she had to cancel their meeting that afternoon—her four o'clock with Pam Withers and her dog Casey.

"I won't be needing your services at this time." The woman sounded upset, but before Maddie could get more information from her or offer her condolences for what sounded like a tragic situation, Pam Withers hung up.

Stunned and disappointed, Maddie removed the appointment from her schedule and sent Patrick a quick message to let him know about the cancellation.

Though she hated to lose a potential client (especially if it was because of an animal's death, which is what Maddie's immediate concern over the cancellation had been), it turned out that Dr. Sheridan's only available appointment was at four o'clock that afternoon, right when she would have been meeting Pam and Casey Withers. At least something was working in Maddie's favor. Sort of.

Now she just had to hope that Dr. Sheridan could fix whatever was affecting Goliath.

CHAPTER NINE

Maddie and Goliath spent twenty-five minutes puttering around the waiting room of East Rogers Park Animal Hospital before being shown into an examining room. Part of the wait was due to Maddie's habit of hyperpunctuality—arriving five minutes early felt like showing up late. But part of the delay, she was informed by the smiling young woman at the front desk, was the result of an emergency case that had thrown off Dr. Sheridan's schedule. The young woman apologized profusely, but Maddie brushed her concerns aside. She understood that such circumstances were an unfortunate reality in veterinary medicine, so she didn't mind. That it gave her an opportunity to explore a little and satisfy some of her curiosity about Dr. Sheridan's practice was just a bonus.

Whoever had designed the waiting area had taken the needs of various animals into serious account. The room was spacious, providing a breadth of territory for pets and their owners, and the walls, painted a soft grayish blue, were adorned with an array of framed pieces. In addition to the usual animal artwork found in veterinarians' offices—captivating photographs, paintings and drawings of dogs and cats in every conceivable pose—Maddie noticed several readers' choice awards from local publications designating Dr. Sheridan and East Rogers Park Animal Hospital as one of the best vet practices in Chicago. Little Guys Pet Care had recently received a similar honor in the dog walking category, and Maddie spent a few minutes skimming one glowing review of Dr. Sheridan's work while Goliath, totally at ease, dozed at her feet. From there, she moved on to some adorable black and white drawings of puppies and kittens by a local artist, but before she got to fully appreciate them, a gangling vet tech who hadn't entirely grasped the concept of shaving beckoned to her.

Once inside the exam room, Goliath sniffed perfunctorily at the baseboards while Maddie answered questions from the scruffy tech, who dutifully wrote everything down. Maddie got the impression that he was either new to his position or just naturally anxious as his sentences were infused with a steady stream of "ums" and his hands fluttered about in the air when he wasn't cracking his knuckles or taking careful notes. By the time he left the room, he'd determined that Goliath had lost three pounds since his last visit and assured Maddie that the doctor would be in shortly.

Doubting his statement—most doctors weren't known for their timeliness—Maddie wondered what was so appealing about this practice. Aside from being shiny and relatively new, it seemed like just about every other veterinary practice she'd ever visited.

Goliath had settled himself comfortably on the floor at Maddie's feet, and she crouched down to give him a thorough petting when the door opened. Instantly, Maddie understood how anyone with functioning eyeballs would be drawn to this doctor over any other vet in the city of Chicago. Dr. Sheridan was gorgeous.

She'd tried to restrain her long, dark chestnut hair, but several strands hung loose around her face, which held more exotic beauty than Maddie had thought possible in someone with the last name Sheridan. Her olive skin seemed to glow, and her intense light brown eyes shone with affection for her patient. Maddie felt invisible as the doctor squealed Goliath's name and breezed past her to sit on the floor and dote on him. Her full lips stretched into a bewitchingly lopsided smile, and as Goliath licked her magnificent face, she laughed and scratched behind his ears. Maddie, wishing she could get such a greeting from the doctor, managed to swallow, thankfully without gulping audibly like a cartoon wolf.

She quickly tidied her unruly ponytail and bemoaned her rumpled attire, the same clothes she had defended as being perfectly acceptable lesbian apparel the night before. As the doctor stood and faced her, Maddie tried unsuccessfully not to stare, but the voluptuous curves beneath Dr. Sheridan's scrubs, coupled with Maddie's lack of female companionship for more than two years, made looking away a Herculean effort.

"Sorry about that," Dr. Sheridan said in a melodious voice. "Goliath and I go way back, and I haven't seen him in a while." She focused those irresistible caramel-colored eyes on Maddie, and after favoring her with a questioning smile, she shook Maddie's hand and introduced herself. A little electric shock traveled from Maddie's hand throughout her body, and she had difficulty remembering her own name. Not trusting her voice, Maddie just smiled and savored the brief contact.

"Where's Howard?" she asked.

The air suddenly left Maddie's lungs. She hadn't considered that she would have to break the news of Howard's death to Goliath's vet, and the sudden weight of that responsibility troubled her deeply. She'd been dealing with the aftermath of Howard's murder for two days, had thought and talked about little else, but with the exception of Gwendolyn, Maddie hadn't broken the news of his death to anyone who knew him. She had no way of knowing just how close Howard and Dr. Sheridan were (or weren't), which somehow made the whole business more daunting. She felt lost in the immensity of the task before her.

"Howard died," Maddie said, almost in a whisper.

"What?" Dr. Sheridan's shock was evident.

Maddie heard the quiver in the doctor's voice, noticed tears gleaming on her lower eyelids and saw that her body trembled. She worried that Dr. Sheridan might pass out, and without thinking, grabbed her by the shoulder and forearm and guided her to the chair in the corner. Although the feel of the doctor's small, firm shoulder and the softness of her skin registered in some tiny part of Maddie's mind, most of her brain wanted to fix things and soothe this woman's sudden distress. Somehow, that translated into giving Dr. Sheridan more information about Howard's death. Before she knew what she was doing, Maddie started babbling. She couldn't help it.

"It was two days ago, in the morning while I was out walking Goliath. I'd been walking him for Howard since he fell down the stairs. Howard, that is, not Goliath. Goliath was fine. We were only gone for twenty minutes, and someone came in, I guess someone he knew—there weren't any signs of a break-in—and used his walking stick, I think, to—" Finally realizing that the gruesome particulars might push the woman over the edge, Maddie opted for the simple, if edited, truth. "Someone killed him."

"He was murdered?" Dr. Sheridan sniffled loudly. Pain and distress were unmistakably etched in both her voice and her horrified expression, and Maddie regretted exposing the doctor, even a tiny bit, to the horror of Howard's demise. "My God. Who would murder a sweet man like Howard?"

Apparently not you, Maddie thought, relieved that she didn't have to add another suspect to her list, especially one she was developing a titanic crush on. "I've been wondering the same thing," she said as she handed the doctor a tissue.

After a few more minutes (and tissues), Dr. Sheridan gradually composed herself and, though shaken, seemed less fragile. Reaching out to stroke her patient's fur, she asked "How is Goliath handling this?"

"That's why we're here."

Maddie explained that Goliath hadn't been eating. As Maddie revealed the pertinent details of the past two days, Dr. Sheridan began her examination, listening to Maddie's story while checking Goliath's eyes and ears, feeling his abdomen, taking his temperature. When Maddie mentioned that she and Goliath had discovered Howard's body, Dr. Sheridan looked at Maddie with sorrow and sympathy before returning her attention to her examination.

"I think he's just depressed, but I need to know that there isn't something wrong. Something other than losing his family and his home," Maddie said after Dr. Sheridan listened to Goliath's heart and lungs and removed the stethoscope from her ears. Dr. Sheridan nodded as she made notes in Goliath's chart. Wanting to rid the room of its hefty silence, Maddie spoke again. "I would have taken him to my regular vet—I go to Dr. Mitra at Ashland Pet Care—but I thought, since you know Goliath, that you might have more insight," she offered as a sort of lame apology for bringing this tragedy to the doctor's attention.

When Dr. Sheridan looked up from her notes, Maddie noticed a subtle change in her demeanor. Her professional persona hung tenuously over the sadness that still peeked out through her eyes, and Maddie suspected that she was relying on that polished bearing to get her through until she could fully grieve away from the prying eyes of a complete stranger.

"You're probably right that Goliath is depressed. He's been through a lot in a short span of time." Gazing at the handsome dog who pressed himself against her thigh, Dr. Sheridan stroked his head and neck, eliciting a little grunt of satisfaction from Goliath. Admiring the doctor's long, strong fingers, Maddie appreciated his delight completely. When Dr. Sheridan finally spoke again, her voice was quiet but confident. "His weight loss is understandable but a little troubling. We need to get him eating and back to his normal weight, so I'm going to send you home with an appetite stimulant, which should get our boy here interested in food again."

Maddie nodded, grateful at the prospect of Goliath's return to normalcy. As much as his independent curiosity had frustrated her in the past, it would be a welcome change from the heartbreaking sadness that he carried with him now.

"Now, even though his mood is the most likely cause of

his loss of appetite, we still need to be sure that there's not something else going on. So far I haven't heard, felt or seen anything out of the ordinary, but if it's all right with you, I'd like to check his blood to eliminate any medical causes."

"Absolutely," Maddie answered readily. "We'll do whatever you think is necessary."

Dr. Sheridan smiled at Maddie's eagerness to help Goliath, and their eyes locked in a lingering gaze. The doctor's gleaming expression thrilled Maddie. She was still basking in the glow of the doctor's approval when Dr. Sheridan summoned the nervous tech to bring Goliath into the back and draw his blood. Goliath padded away with his escort, as happy as if he were headed to the park or the beach, and Maddie marveled at how content he was at the vet's office.

Once they were alone, Dr. Sheridan continued, "Since we're operating on the assumption that Goliath is depressed, not ill, you should try to keep him more active and engaged. Lots of exercise. If there's anything at all that he takes pleasure in right now, do that as much as possible, and reward him when he shows signs of happiness, but no fussing over him or offering treats to cheer him up when he's sad. You don't want to encourage his depression by rewarding him when he's moping."

"So, basically, I need to train him to be happy again?"

"That's one way to put it." The doctor grinned, and Maddie felt relief that she was becoming more than a dark cloud over this woman's entire day. Before Maddie could think of another comment to raise Dr. Sheridan's spirits further, maybe even make her laugh, the doctor returned her focus to Goliath's condition. "I will call with the results from the blood work tomorrow. Can I get your contact information?"

As she wrote down her name and number, Maddie reflected with resigned disappointment that the first time that a beautiful woman had asked for her number in years it had, of course, been about a dog rather than the attraction she wished existed between them.

The doctor scanned the information Maddie had given her. "Is this the best number to reach you at?"

"Yes, it's my cell number."

"So I won't be bothering your roommate or…anyone?"

It took a moment for the underlying meaning of the doctor's question to register with Maddie, but once it did, she had a hard time containing her joy. "No. There's no one you need to worry about, Dr. Sheridan."

"It's Nadia." Her gorgeous lips curved up in that endearing lopsided grin she'd shown earlier, and she shook Maddie's hand again. Nadia's hand was warm and soft, and Maddie was pleased at the duration of their contact. The doctor seemed as reluctant to pull her hand away as Maddie.

"I will definitely call you tomorrow, Miss Smithwick."

Instead of correcting the mispronunciation of her name, Maddie said, "Call me Maddie."

CHAPTER TEN

On the walk home, Maddie felt better than she had in days, possibly weeks. She was buoyant, giddy almost, as if the last, wonderful hour had magically fixed her life. It had certainly alleviated some of her concerns, and now she felt oddly cheery. It was ridiculous for her to feel so happy. There was no guarantee that the appetite stimulant would work, though she would find out soon enough since the vet tech had administered Goliath's first dose before they left. Nor could she be certain that playing with Goliath would raise his spirits, but she felt hopeful about his well-being now, and she appreciated the expertise and gentle care that Dr. Sheridan provided.

And what about the doctor? Maddie really didn't know what to make of their exchange at the end of Goliath's appointment. The optimist in her wanted to believe that Dr. Sheridan—Nadia—had been flirting with her, but Maddie's rich history of beautiful women ignoring her or, worse, thinking of her as a good friend and nothing more, led Maddie to the conclusion that her inner optimist was also a sadist. It elevated Maddie with delicious expectation and then howled with amusement as rejection sent her crashing back to earth. But it felt so good to believe that she was desirable—even after spending several hours roaming the neighborhood in the heat and the one thousand percent humidity that still engulfed the city—that she thought she might try to keep her doubts at bay for a while. She had enough distractions to occupy her mind for at least another hour.

Now that her love life might have been resurrected and Goliath was likely on the road to recovery, Maddie had only two issues battling it out for the top spot on her list of concerns: Howard's murder and Granny Doyle's health. Maddie's mother had sent a text (an act that always surprised Maddie) after arriving at Granny's hospital room (at exactly noon, when Granny said she would be allowed to enter, Maddie suspected). She reread what her mother had written: "The doctors still haven't made any progress. If we don't get some answers soon, we may have to start visiting your grandmother in prison."

The weirdness of her mother texting was mitigated somewhat by her insistence on proper grammar and spelling, and Maddie chuckled in spite of her growing frustration with the situation. There was nothing that she could do, aside from calling, visiting and worrying, and if she let her mind dwell on her grandmother for too long, she would start to panic.

A much saner use of her brain power was to focus on Howard's murder. Unlike the other two topics she'd decided not to think about, this situation, with its ever-fluctuating list of suspects, seemed just as hopeless, but at least she could ponder and puzzle over it without losing her mind to insecurity or worries. Half of her—the same half that was often tempted to peek at the crossword puzzle answer key—wished that Detective Fitzwilliam would solve the case, arrest the murderer and call her with the good news. For all she knew, he already had caught the killer and hadn't called her because he had no reason to. From a police standpoint, the identity of Howard's killer was none of her business, unless Dottie was right for a change and they actually believed that Maddie was the murderer. Since she hadn't been arrested, she had to assume that wasn't the case, and since Detective Fitzwilliam had already made his feelings about her investigative help perfectly clear, that meant that if she wanted to know who did it, she'd have to figure it out herself.

And if she was going to do that, then she needed to know why three members of Dottie's dog show group had hated Howard. Right now, her best chance of finding that out would be Dottie. Her input about Adam, Albert and Ruth might prove vital to solving the case, so Maddie knew how badly she needed to get back into Dottie's good graces.

Preoccupied, she let Goliath wander in whatever direction pleased him. She paid little attention to their route, knowing that she could easily find her way back home. But by the time Maddie realized where Goliath was headed, where he would habitually go after leaving Dr. Sheridan's office, it was too late. They were already there.

She looked up at Howard's house. She had thought there would be an indication that a brutal murder had been committed, some sign that, on this spot, life for Howard, Goliath and herself had changed irrevocably. But there was nothing, not even police tape. It looked just like it always had, a thought that made Maddie unaccountably sad. Downhearted and probably confused at the sight of his now off-limits house, Goliath released a mournful sigh and settled himself on the sidewalk at Maddie's feet. With a second hopeless, shuddering sigh, he rested his chin on his front paws and stared forlornly at his former home.

Maddie's heart sank further. She immediately thought that this was probably the opposite of what Dr. Sheridan had advised and was wondering how to get him away from there without using treats when a short, lean whippet of a man with a full head of graying hair bustled past her and crouched before the despondent canine sprawled on the sidewalk.

"Goliath?" he cried in a voice much deeper than Maddie had expected. "Is that really you? No one knew where you went after—we were so worried." As his words rolled out in a continuous stream, the man petted Goliath vigorously, behavior which Goliath seemed to endure rather than enjoy.

The man apparently believed that Goliath had teleported to this spot as he paid no attention to Goliath's leash or the person at the other end of it, so Maddie asked, "You two know each other?"

At that, the man stood bolt upright and focused his considerable energies on Maddie.

"Where are my manners?" He slapped his forehead. "I'm Lester Parrish, Howard's neighbor. I'm sure you heard about me from Howard. I live on the top floor of that three-flat there." He pointed to the building adjacent to Howard's lot. "I've been there for twenty-five years, and I've seen everyone and everything come and go. Oh, the stories I could tell you. You're the dog walker. Mavis, right?" He didn't even pause for Maddie to answer. "I've seen you with Goliath, and Howard told me all about you. Did you take Goliath in? I'm so relieved. I was worried sick about this little devil."

Maddie felt certain that Lester Parrish practiced circular breathing in order to speak so much—incessantly, really—without fainting from lack of oxygen. His words continued to pour forth as she pondered his impressive gift of oration. Since she doubted she'd ever get the chance to utter a single syllable, she considered calculating Lester's words per minute.

Meanwhile Lester changed topics and was now regaling Maddie with the intimate details of his neighbors' lives. The couple across the street would never make it, Lester assured her, because they both had wandering eyes. The old lady up the street was a kleptomaniac. She'd even stolen a garden gnome from a house down the block. And Lester's downstairs neighbor, who worked for Streets and Sanitation, was cheating the city and the taxpayers.

"He's been on disability for months, but he's healthy enough to play basketball in the park every day. I've called to report his abuse of the system, but nothing's been done, of course. They call this the city that works. What a joke. Our parks are filthy. The streets are more pothole than pavement. Every employee at the City Clerk's Office is on perpetual lunch break, and the cops spend more time reading the paper in their cars—that we pay for, of course—than out working to keep us safe. I tell you, the only thing this city is working is my last nerve."

Overcoming the mental fog that had settled right about the time that Lester introduced himself, Maddie realized he could be an excellent source of information if only she could steer him in the right direction.

She broke in during a miraculous pause. "Were you home on that day?" She lowered her voice to a conspiratorial whisper. "The day that Howard died?"

"I was. I'm retired, so I'm always around. Anyway, I heard the ruckus and thought, 'Here we go again. Just like last time.'"

"Last time?" Maddie jumped in.

"His so-called accident on the stairs that landed him in that wheelchair."

"What? I thought Howard fell down the stairs?"

"Oh, Mavis, he fell all right, but I think he had a little help, if you know what I mean. Or maybe he tripped trying to get away from her." Maddie wondered who Lester meant but had no opportunity to ask. "I tell you, when I heard all that racket, I thought it must be that nasty ex-wife of his back for another round."

"Shelly? Did she come by often?"

"Often enough. She was here every couple of weeks like clockwork to browbeat Howard over something, usually money. She said he owed her."

"It was definitely Shelly that you heard?"

"Oh, I couldn't say for sure. It was an angry person, so I just put two and two together."

Feeling herself getting lost in the tangled web of Lester's story, Maddie needed some clarity. "Was this the day that, you know?"

"Oh, no. This was the first time, a few weeks ago. I thought it was just another one of their fights until the ambulance pulled up in front of Howard's house. So the next time, I called 911 as soon as I heard the fighting start. Not that it did any good. By the time the police decided to show up, Howard was dead, and his killer was gone. I'm sure Howard's tragedy came in the middle of Crossword Puzzle Hour or some vital coffee drinking. The city that works, my foot! I tell you, Mavis, the only thing this city is working—"

"Is your last nerve," Maddie finished his signature line for him. "Goliath and I have to get going. It was really great to meet you." She excused herself, but Lester didn't seem to notice. He chattered away as Maddie got Goliath moving and made her retreat, her mind spinning.

At least one of her questions (possibly the least important one) had been answered. Now she knew who called the police, but nothing else made sense. Why would Howard lie about falling down the stairs? Why cover up for someone? Why didn't he press charges against his assailant? If the person he argued with before his tumble down the stairs was the same person who'd murdered him, it might have saved his life. And what about Shelly? Perhaps she wasn't as busy as she'd led Maddie to believe. If that was the case, then Shelly was back on the suspect list.

Even though it frustrated Maddie to go backward in her investigation, she thought Dottie would be pleased to know that Shelly might not be innocent after all, information that would put Maddie back in Dottie's good graces much faster than flowers. As she and Goliath entered her blessedly air-conditioned home, Maddie called to invite Dottie to dinner.

Her friend answered just before the call went to voice mail. "Hello, darling."

Maddie cringed at the "darling," the term of indifference Gwendolyn had used with all of her husbands shortly before they became her ex-husbands. Granny might be right about Dottie's affection for Maddie eventually triumphing over her indignation, but it didn't look like that would be happening any time soon. Maddie decided to plow ahead anyway.

"What are your plans for this evening?"

"Why? Did you want to tag along and alienate more of my associates?"

Maddie supposed she deserved that. After all, Dottie had gone to great lengths to help her, and Maddie had shown her appreciation by insulting Dottie's friends during an intense argument with one of them. Even though she knew Dottie would milk this grudge indefinitely, deciding to move on only after some landmark of contrition known only to Dottie had been reached, Maddie apologized once more.

"I really am sorry, Dottie. I shouldn't have treated your guests that way. There's no defense for my rudeness, but I hope you'll let me start making amends with dinner tonight."

A reluctant, sighing "Hmmm" was Dottie's only reply, but Maddie thought her friend sounded more curious than upset. She cursed herself for engendering optimism with her earlier thoughts of Nadia.

"I have some news to share," she added, hoping to hook Dottie by triggering her nosiness.

"It's rather late notice," Dottie stated noncommittally. "But perchance I can make myself available for your atonement. What did you have in mind to try to regain my undying devotion?"

"We can have anything you'd like," Maddie said, relieved that Dottie was at least willing to start the lengthy process of forgiveness.

"Can it be lobster?" Dottie asked, sounding less irritated still.

"I'm allergic to shellfish," Maddie reminded her friend.

"I'm not."

"Fine. I'll court anaphylactic shock as an act of penance, but if we end the night in the emergency room, don't say I didn't warn you."

After the barest of pauses, Dottie asked, "How does seven work for you?"

CHAPTER ELEVEN

Maddie really wanted to catch up on some of her work, so in the snippet of time she had before Dottie's arrival, she headed back to Little Guys and the backlog of tasks that awaited her.

The first thing she encountered was a note from Patrick. "We got a couple of weird calls while you were out. No urgency, but I thought you should know. We can discuss tomorrow. P.S.—I hope all is well with Goliath."

Even though he said it wasn't urgent, Maddie was curious to find out what qualified as a "weird call" in Patrick's world— amusing wrong numbers or heavy-breathing dog collar fetishists? She grabbed her cell phone to check in with him, a good idea anyway since they'd barely crossed paths in the last three days, but her business line rang at the same time. Curiosity would have to wait.

"Are you the dog walker who murdered her client?" a harsh voice asked. Stunned, she barely squeaked out a feeble "No" before the caller hung up.

Shock quickly gave way to investigative curiosity. From all of the detective shows she'd watched over the years, she assumed the call must have been the killer trying to throw her off her game, a sign that she was getting close to something. Little did the killer know, Maddie felt about as close to solving this mystery as the Cubs were to winning the World Series. If only Maddie was as skilled a detective as the killer seemed to believe she was, she might be able to start eliminating suspects instead of adding them. Still, she was oddly buoyed by the harassment. If the killer was trying to warn her off, then maybe she was closer to the truth than she realized. She again reflected on what she knew and pondered it in the context of this case.

A select number of people knew about Howard's death, and even fewer knew of her connection to it. To make that small group even smaller, Maddie automatically eliminated her mother, her grandmother and Dottie from the list of people who would call to harass her. Considering further (and less with her head than with other parts of her anatomy), she also ruled out Dr. Sheridan. That left Howard's ex-wife and the three members of Dottie's dog group who had no love for Howard. She again felt buoyed by the fact that her list hadn't grown in size. Hopefully she could narrow it down some after talking to Dottie about Adam, Albert and Ruth, and of course, discovering the identity of her mystery caller would also lead her in the right direction. Unfortunately, the caller's voice would be no of help to Maddie—even if she had known any of her suspects' voices well enough to recognize them over the phone, it wouldn't have mattered because it sounded like the caller had been trying to disguise his or her normal speaking voice.

Contacting Patrick for details of the weird calls he'd mentioned might prove helpful. He answered on the second ring.

"Hey boss." Patrick sounded cheery, as always. "I wasn't expecting to hear from you tonight. I hope my note didn't scare you."

"Scare isn't the word I'd use. Do you have a minute to share the details?"

"Sure," he answered without hesitation. Maddie figured he was on his way to the gym, his usual evening endeavor, but he willingly put his workout on hold to help her out. For the billionth time in a week, she thanked the Fates for sending her Patrick.

"It was in the late afternoon when the crew was turning in keys and wrapping up the day. Oh, Hannah needs another policy reminder, by the way."

"Texting again?"

"Afraid so. I guess because I only walk Peanut three days a week, she forgot I'd be in the area when she walked Ralphie. I caught her in the act."

Maddie groaned and made a note to meet with her newest and most policy-resistant employee. Maddie was fairly laid-back as far as policies went, but she insisted that her walkers not distract themselves with technology at any time that an animal was in their care. Though some of her employees pushed back, Maddie didn't think it was too much to ask people to focus on the work she paid them to do. Since the safety and well-being of animals depended on that focus and it only lasted for twenty to thirty minutes at a time, she refused to back down. If an employee couldn't comply with the rules, that employee could be replaced.

"Anyway," Patrick in his typical ricochet style, returned to the matter at hand. "We got a call, and at first I thought we got another new client. I was really excited until he asked how many of our customers have died. Not a standard question, but not completely off-the-wall either, or so I thought, because I assumed he meant animals." A knot of queasiness settled in the pit of Maddie's stomach, and she wished she had a remote control for her life, that she could just change the channel to something more pleasant, like a rerun of *I Love Lucy* or something. "When I started to explain that some pets have died while they've been our clients but that none have died while they were directly in our care, he interrupted to say he meant people, not animals. That threw me a little, so I asked what this was about. That's when he hung up. I got two more calls like that within an hour."

Maddie contemplated the details Patrick offered, latching on to a hopefully significant element of his story.

"So it was a man who called?"

Patrick hesitated. "I can't say for sure, boss. The even weirder part is that it seemed like whoever called was trying to disguise his voice. Or hers."

Frustrated that Patrick hadn't had better luck than her in determining the gender of the caller, Maddie held out hope that he might have picked out some identifying feature.

"I know you said it was disguised, but was there anything about the caller's voice that stood out, even a little?" Maddie knew she was grasping at straws.

"Sorry boss. It was so quick and so weird. I couldn't say."

"That's okay, Patrick. Don't worry about it."

After reassuring him twice more that he shouldn't be concerned about the calls and that he'd handled the situation as well as could be expected, Maddie finally got him to hang up and get back to his evening. Though she hadn't really expected Patrick to provide the identity of the caller and solve the mystery for her, it was somewhat disheartening that she couldn't glean a single clue from the information that he gave her. Even more disturbing (but still somewhat satisfying) was that the caller had escalated the harassment when Maddie had answered, as if he—or she—had been hoping to intimidate Maddie all along.

Glancing at her watch, Maddie saw that she had only thirty minutes to get some work done before she needed to head home and get ready for Dottie's arrival, hardly enough time to accomplish anything worthwhile. By the time she got started on any of the tasks before her, she'd have to stop. She sighed in resignation at the continued accumulation of work she would face, assuming she ever got to return her focus to her business.

CHAPTER TWELVE

"Did we interrupt your in-home hazmat training?" Dottie and Anastasia stood on Maddie's front porch, Anastasia staring quizzically at Maddie (though it really didn't seem like it should be possible for a dog to infuse her gaze with so much mocking bewilderment). Dottie stared too, her eyes flicking up and down, taking in the curious appearance of her best friend.

Maddie wore her raincoat with the hood up, rubber gloves and safety goggles, all to protect herself from Dottie's dinner, and she wasn't even preparing the food. Not that she couldn't cook, though no one would mistake her for a great chef. Granny Doyle had taught her a few things (not the recipe for her famous no-raisin oatmeal cookies, regrettably). Living alone and fending for herself had taught her the rest, so she could find her way around a kitchen with satisfying results. However, the thought of plunging a living creature into a pot of boiling water was unbearable to her, so she'd ordered dinner from a local restaurant. All she had to do was transfer the food to a plate, but still she had covered almost every inch of her skin in order to safely handle her edible apology to Dottie.

"You look ridiculous," Dottie declared as she and Anastasia breezed past Maddie and headed straight to the kitchen. Normally Dottie would help herself to a cocktail, but this evening she lingered close by Maddie's liquor cabinet, waiting for Maddie to offer her a drink. Obviously she was in full wounded princess mode.

"True," Maddie agreed as she entered the kitchen where Anastasia and the boys sniffed one another cordially before making themselves comfortable in and around Bart's dog bed. Maddie wasn't sure if it was chivalrous behavior on Bart and Goliath's part or pampered expectation on Anastasia's, but it amused her to see Anastasia in the bed flanked on both sides by the boys, who were splayed on the floor. "But," Maddie continued, "at least my throat won't close before I get to share my big news."

She'd almost said "Before I get the chance to properly grovel before you," but had thankfully stopped herself. Even though Dottie and Maddie both knew that's what was happening, acknowledging it would set the whole process back at least a day. The act of wooing Dottie worked best when all parties involved ignored the fact that it was taking place.

Turning to Dottie, who attempted to convey disinterest in Maddie's news, Maddie made the awaited drink offer. Although she anticipated that her friend would order up some insane cocktail that no one had consumed since before Prohibition, she was pleasantly surprised when Dottie requested a martini. Given her years of experience, Maddie could make martinis for Dottie in her sleep.

As Maddie set about mixing their drinks, Dottie settled herself at the table and, still trying not to appear too eager, asked, "So you said you had some news? Do tell."

Maddie drew out the suspense unintentionally, focused as she was on carrying Dottie's cocktail and plate of poison to the table. She answered once the threat was safely out of her hands. "I ran into Howard's neighbor while Goliath and I were walking home from his vet appointment."

"Oh, what did the doctor have to say?"

"Can I tell one story at a time, please?"

"Pardon me," Dottie intoned melodramatically. "Carry on, by all means," she commanded with a theatrical flourish of her hand.

Maddie sputtered in quiet exasperation as she removed her layers of protective gear. She grabbed her own dinner and drink and joined Dottie before resuming her story. "The neighbor, Lester Parrish—I don't think I've ever met a bigger gossipmonger—told me that he didn't think Howard fell down the stairs, at least not without some assistance, and he suggested that Shelly Monk might have been the one to help him take that tumble."

"I knew she did it!"

"She might not have done anything, Dottie. Speculation from the male Gladys Kravitz isn't exactly rock-solid evidence."

"Don't count on it, lemon drop. That woman is evil."

"I agree that she's unpleasant." Dottie's eyebrow arched upward in a wry expression of disbelief that spoke volumes. "Extremely unpleasant," Maddie amended. "But that doesn't make her a murderer."

Dottie harrumphed but otherwise remained silent as Maddie conveyed the remainder of Lester Parrish's observations, at least what was relevant. As prone to rubbernecking as Dottie could be, Maddie doubted that she would care about Lester's garden-gnome-thieving elderly neighbor.

"I still say she did it."

"I'll pass your considered opinion on to Detective Fitzwilliam."

"I'm certain that he could benefit from a bit of direction."

"Meaning?"

"That idiot Detective Fitzwilliam interrogated every member of the owners group today."

"Even Ruth?" Maddie risked broaching the sticking point between them.

Dottie's solemn nod served as her reply.

"I hope he survived," Maddie muttered.

"He frittered away valuable hours cross-examining each of us, asking ridiculous, useless questions regarding our relationships with Howard, our whereabouts at the time of his...departure, what we knew about that monstrous trophy. On and on he went, getting nowhere, I'm sure. What a colossal waste of time."

"Why is that a waste of his time when yesterday that was how I was going to crack the case wide open?"

"Because after you probed the inner workings of everyone's hearts and minds, we now know that none of my fellow purebred aficionados could have had anything to do with the misfortune that befell Howard."

"Well..." Maddie spoke cautiously, still not sure the subject was safe to discuss. But since Dottie had brought it up, she couldn't very well ignore the opening.

"You mean you suspect one of my comrades?" Dottie sounded shocked, even though it had been *her* grand plan to investigate her friends.

"Three actually."

"I don't know if I should be appalled that someone I associate with could be a murderer, proud that my plan worked or pleased that you managed to get some sleuthing done before you alienated the entire gathering."

"If you divulge some of your friends' secrets, then you can add 'magnanimous' to that list of descriptors."

"Am I the Watson to your Holmes? The Hastings to your Poirot? The Nora to your Nick?" Dottie seemed a little too delighted by the prospect of being a temporary sidekick.

"If you can tell me why Adam Whelan, Albert Silver and Ruth Charles hated Howard, then you can be the whomever you choose to the whatever you want to call me."

Dottie's eyes twinkled at the possibilities, and Maddie wished she'd phrased her answer more carefully. "With Ruth and Howard, it seemed like things just fell apart. I wish I could say why."

"You mean Ruth actually got along with Howard?" Maddie wanted to add, "Or anyone?" but resisted the urge.

"They were the best of friends, practically inseparable right from the moment of Howard's introduction to the group." Maddie shuddered at the thought of being Ruth Charles' boon companion. "Then a few weeks ago, they had a falling out. Neither one of them would discuss the details, but Howard immediately pulled Goliath from The Boarding School."

"What's The Boarding School?"

"It's a luxury day spa for dogs. There's a trainer and a play palace, and the dogs are pampered mercilessly. They offer massages, Reiki, mud baths." Maddie made a mental note to check the place out both for the case and for business ideas. "Ruth introduced us all to it—Anastasia goes every Wednesday, and she adores it. She simply glows when Raphael brings her home. She—"

Dottie must have caught Maddie's withering glare because she abruptly returned to the point. "After his tiff with Ruth, Howard stopped sending Goliath to The Boarding School. He said he wanted to keep him close, that he'd feel safer with Goliath nearby."

"That obviously worked out." Maddie wondered what had happened between Ruth and Howard, but doubted she would learn the truth by asking Ruth. She wouldn't even tell Dottie what had happened, so what hope did Maddie have of getting the story out of her? Maybe she would be lucky enough to solve the case without that piece of information, which seemed highly likely since she'd caught so many breaks so far. "What about Adam and Albert? What did they have against Howard?"

"The trouble with them started about a year ago when Howard claimed that Adam 'got a little fresh' with him at an event. No one believed him, of course."

"Why not?"

"You've seen Howard, and you've seen Albert. If you weren't so devoted to the X chromosome, who would you choose?" Maddie had to agree that Howard would not have won a beauty competition against Albert Silver. "And from what I've surmised, Albert's bank account is even more attractive. He's so charming, gallant, intelligent. The whole package, really. If not for the gay thing, he'd make a wonderful number four. I could give your grandmother the wedding she requested." Dottie smiled to herself in dreamy contemplation of this idea. "Speaking of which, how is your grandmother?"

"Ready to kill half the medical staff at the hospital if she doesn't get an explanation soon, but otherwise the same."

"The poor dear. Are you planning to visit her tomorrow?" Maddie nodded, worrisome thoughts of her grandmother filling her head. "I'll join you to help revivify her."

"She would love that."

"Consider it done. Not too early though."

"Of course not," Maddie agreed, looking forward to the visit even though she knew her grandmother and best friend would most likely gang up on her. Maddie hated to admit it, but the teasing she was in for when Granny and Dottie joined forces likely would lift Granny's spirits, and if it would help Granny feel better, then Maddie could endure a little good-natured mockery. "Back to Adam and Albert. They hated Howard because he said that Adam hit on him?"

"No, pet, that was merely the genesis of their ill will. After that humiliation, Howard went after the boys."

"He went after them? In what way?" Maddie couldn't imagine Howard resorting to violence, nor could she picture him as a malicious man, even though she'd already heard a similar tale from his ex-wife.

"He intervened, shall we say, in a number of Albert's real estate deals. Albert lost out on quite a bit of money. But I haven't heard anything about their warfare in months. I thought that had all died down."

"Maybe it died down," Maddie said softly, feeling the impact of this new information. She was slowly getting used to the unpalatable side of Howard Monk. "Or maybe it escalated."

"How will you figure that out?"

"I guess I'll start by talking to Adam and Albert, assuming that's possible after yesterday's tirade."

"Don't worry about that, ladybug. I told everyone that you'd recently suffered a blow to the head and couldn't be held responsible for your ridiculous ramblings. They were all supremely sympathetic. Except for Ruth, of course."

"Thank you for that," Maddie said wryly, hoping Dottie's dog show cohorts understood her penchant for embellishment.

"I help in whatever way I can, sugar foot," Dottie beamed.

"It's truly appreciated."

Bart snored softly, drawing Dottie's attention to the pack.

"How is Goliath?" His ears twitched at the sound of his name, and Dottie scrutinized him. "He seems less glum, but that might be the therapeutic influence of my Anastasia. She has a rejuvenating effect on most creatures, you know."

Maddie looked at the three dogs who still lay in a content, peaceful herd. Goliath sighed and rested his chin on his paws, staring at Maddie with his sad eyes. He looked pretty much the same to her, but he had eaten a couple of bites earlier. She had hope he was improving.

"The doctor took some blood to rule out anything physical, but she thinks he's just depressed."

"You needed a doctor for that insight? I could have told you that and you wouldn't have had to waste your time."

"It wasn't a total waste. She gave me some good advice and some meds for him. And I think she's a lesbian."

"Why the uncertainty? Gaydar on the fritz?"

"It's not like she had a rainbow stamped on her forehead."

"Did she do the secret handshake?" Dottie smiled, pleased with herself.

Tired of rolling her eyes and almost at the end of her patience, Maddie ignored her friend's comments. "Either she was hitting on me, or I was being uncharacteristically optimistic."

"Do you know how to tell if you've been MIA from the dating world for far too long? You can no longer tell when women are hitting on you."

"It was kind of vague," Maddie offered.

"Give me the details and I will decide." Dottie seemed almost as excited by the possibility of a romantic entanglement with the doctor as Maddie was.

"She told me to call her Nadia."

"Is that actually her name, or was she speaking in some sort of lesbian code?"

Maddie glared at Dottie and otherwise ignored the question. "And then when we shook hands, she held on a little longer than necessary."

"Hmmm. A possible fake name and a lingering handshake. It does seem inconclusive."

"Thank you for that revelation, oh mighty romance wizard." Since their friendship seemed to be back on steady ground, Maddie risked sarcasm. "What do I do?"

"Is she attractive?"

"Like one of those high-powered magnets that lifts cars."

"Well then, when she calls about Goliath's blood work, you'll just have to charm her." Dottie paused as if considering something. "*Can* you charm her?"

"I guess we'll find out tomorrow." But in all honesty, given her track record with women, Maddie feared she already knew the answer.

CHAPTER THIRTEEN

Maddie's first thought upon waking was actually "Thank god it's Friday." She had just endured one of the most difficult weeks of her adult life, so it was justified, but thinking in clichés still rankled, especially when they didn't even apply to her. Considering how far she'd fallen behind in her work, she couldn't justify taking two full days of leisure time until she got herself caught up. And if today ran as smoothly as the last three, then she doubted she'd make much headway, which meant that the impending weekend would be full of work for her.

Even with the burden of a full schedule Maddie stayed in bed and contemplated the day ahead. In addition to the backlog of paperwork, she remembered that she needed to have a talk with Hannah before her walks started. Reprimanding employees was Maddie's least favorite aspect of her job, which was saying a lot seeing as a big part of her chosen profession involved picking up poop with nothing but a thin piece of plastic between her hand and it. Thankfully, she rarely had to deal with recalcitrant employees, so once her conversation with Hannah was over, it would likely be months before she would have to be a disciplinarian again.

On top of that, she and Dottie had agreed to visit Granny at eleven. Maddie had tried for an earlier meeting time, but Dottie refused to entertain thoughts of rising "early." In her opinion, Maddie was lucky she'd agreed to appear before noon. So eleven it was. In spite of her initial disappointment with the time, Maddie now realized that it worked in her favor. She really wanted to go running—she'd skipped her morning run the last two days, and her body craved the activity. Thanks to Dottie's lackadaisical approach to mornings, Maddie had a better chance of squeezing in a run and still getting some work done before heading to the hospital.

Given the early hour, it was probably still cool enough to take Bart with her—the sun wouldn't truly start baking them until seven-thirty or eight o'clock. However, one glance at the corner where Bart and Goliath lay curled up together (so close that Bart's shaggy fur fluttered in the breeze from Goliath's breath) told Maddie that Goliath would benefit from Bart's company more than she would.

She got herself out of bed and padded toward the kitchen for a light breakfast and some necessary coffee. She should probably be mainlining coffee this morning thanks to her late night—Dottie had left just five hours earlier, and Maddie had stayed up another hour cleaning her kitchen and taking the boys for a late-night walk around the neighborhood. At the very least, she should try to sleep a little longer, but once she was out of bed, going back to sleep was hopeless. Fortunately for her, the run would be invigorating. Running almost always was, and if she was quick, she could put in four miles and still get to work early enough to do some catching up. Maybe her weekend wouldn't be totally shot after all.

Within twenty-five minutes she was out the door, having fed the boys (cheerfully noting Goliath's interest in his meal) and let them into the yard to take care of business. When she was sure they were comfortable and happy (or as close to it as

Goliath was getting these days), Maddie headed out the door, eager for physical exertion.

Heading east toward the lake, she watched the sun climb, a fiery ball staining the morning sky a vivid pinkish orange. Farther west, the deep blue of the night still clung to the sky, but by the time Maddie wrapped up her run, the dazzling blue of what she expected to be a gorgeous but hot day would be in full effect.

The scenery only got more beautiful once she reached the lakefront trail, an eighteen-mile paved path that skirted the lake shore. For much of her run she could glance east and see the lake, sunlight dancing across its surface. At other times, the lush green trees of the parks obscured her view of the water. The natural beauty of the city—something so few expected to find in Chicago—surrounded her as she put in the miles. She suspected that the biggest attraction for most users was the path's convenience, but she hoped that the scenery was a draw for at least some of the other runners, cyclists and even the dreaded roller bladers. Though runners and cyclists (some of whom rode like they were racing in a velodrome rather than sharing a narrow path with scores of sometimes oblivious pedestrians) often butted heads over shared use of the trail, the one thing they could all agree on was that roller bladers should be shot, or at least banned from the path.

One day, Maddie wanted to run the entire length of the lakefront trail. She thought it would be fun to start at the southernmost point and make her way home. She'd have to take a cab to Seventy-first Street where the path terminated because no one she knew would understand her desire or be willing to get up early enough to drive her there and leave her to run all the way home.

Abruptly she wondered if the fact that her idea of a fun time was an eighteen-mile run for the hell of it had any bearing on her perpetually single status. But maybe that situation would change today when Dr. Sheridan called. As soon as that thought entered her head, Maddie laughed at herself. She didn't even know for certain if Dr. Sheridan was a lesbian, and she surely didn't know if she was really interested in Maddie, yet she was already partnering them off. Since when was she so desperate for romance? Maybe Granny and Dottie were right—she needed to get out more.

She saw a few other runners and smiled or nodded in acknowledgement of their shared interest. Most of them wore headphones, and some even carried their phones with them. To Maddie that was blasphemy. She ran not only for her health and fitness but also because it's how she found peace and freedom. Being attached to her cell phone would eliminate that. As for running with music, although she understood that some people needed a beat to encourage them, or they needed something to distract them from the eternal reckoning of miles travelled versus miles remaining, to Maddie it was like running blindfolded. She didn't need the external motivation, and she preferred to hear when someone or something was coming up behind her. Safety concerns aside, she loved the sounds of the city, especially this early when it was just waking up. She was surrounded by chattering squirrels, chirping birds and the rustling of leaves overhead stirring in the breeze. Who needed a good beat when your surroundings were so inspiring?

Of course, without music to distract her, Maddie's mind sometimes wandered, playing over whatever issues were prominent in her life, like now. Her brain raced with thoughts of last night's conversation with Dottie. Knowing the point of contention between Howard and Ruth would certainly aid Maddie's investigation, and she was disappointed that neither one of them had had the foresight to confide in Dottie, thus making Maddie's life a little easier. She really didn't want to speak to Ruth again, but that was her only option if she couldn't figure out why Ruth had been so angry with Howard.

Given Ruth's opinion of Goliath and Howard's decision to keep his dog at home with him, Maddie felt certain that the troubles between those two had centered on Goliath. But what were the particulars? Why would Ruth call him a "menace"? Had Goliath attacked Ruth's dog? That hardly seemed likely since Goliath was one of the least aggressive dogs Maddie had ever met, but she couldn't imagine what else he might have done to upset Ruth so much. She needed more information and feared that the only way she would get it was by asking Ruth, an option about as appealing to her as skinny-dipping in a vat of hydrochloric acid.

She could always delay the horror of an interaction with Ruth by starting with the two other members of the group who felt no remorse over Howard's brutal end. Maddie hadn't gotten a chance to talk to Albert before Dottie's special sleuthing operation had fallen apart, but she wanted to hear his thoughts on Howard. She had a hard time believing that their spat with Howard would have led to murder, but she knew that people had been killed for less valid reasons (if there could really ever be a valid reason for murder) than money and jealousy. She had an idea about how she could get the men to meet with her, and based on her conversation with Adam, as well as Dottie's great regard for Albert, Maddie hoped her time might even be pleasant as well as fruitful. However, if her efforts to investigate Adam and Albert led nowhere, then she would resign herself to dealing with Ruth unless she could figure out another way to put that conversation off.

Staving off further thoughts of Ruth, Maddie suddenly realized that she'd gone farther than she intended. At this point she had added at least another mile to her original goal. She would have to hurry if she wanted to get to work early enough to accomplish anything, so she turned her thoughts away from homicide and murder suspects and tried to focus on getting home quickly.

No sooner had she made that decision than thoughts of talking to Dr. Sheridan again bombarded her brain with pleasure and terror, in roughly equal measure. Learning the results of Goliath's blood work and any changes to his care she might have to make would alleviate a good portion of Maddie's stress. And then there was the other matter she wished to resolve— the question of Dr. Sheridan's interest in Maddie. However, the idea of successfully flirting with the doctor filled Maddie with doubt and trepidation. Nevertheless, she picked up the pace as she headed home to prepare for the day ahead.

CHAPTER FOURTEEN

"You're late." Dottie's voice echoed across the near-empty lobby. She stood with her hands on her hips, wearing a smug expression. "I almost called upon the National Guard to form a search party."

Maddie glanced at her watch, shook her head, and rolled her eyes simultaneously. "I'm two minutes late. That hardly constitutes a national crisis."

"Angel, you're never late. You are, in fact, disgustingly punctual. What gives?"

"I got held up at work." Maddie didn't want to relive her rotten morning, so she hoped her vague response would satisfy Dottie. Of course it didn't. Dottie's raised eyebrows and arms folded across her chest clearly told Maddie she'd need to offer more details, but when Maddie remained silent, Dottie pressed her for additional information.

"I got up early for this."

"Ten in the morning is only early to undergrads," Maddie said.

"I arrived before you, an event that, in the course of our relationship, has never once occurred and should therefore be rewarded. You owe me, so spill."

"Fine." Maddie launched into the story of her morning as they headed toward the elevators.

After rushing to complete her run that morning, Maddie had made the time-management mistake of bringing Bart and Goliath to work with her. At the time it had seemed like a great way to keep them engaged and content—Bart loved all the activity and attention he received whenever he was a working dog. She also thought it would be a great way to keep an eye on Goliath, which was, by extension, a great way to convince herself that she was obsessing over Dr. Sheridan's call out of concern for Goliath's well-being rather than any personal benefit.

But Maddie hadn't factored in Goliath's propensity for lingering over every bush, flower, or blade of grass whenever they walked together. He seemed to take pleasure in his ritual sniffing, so she didn't want to rush him, even though she was in a hurry. Worse though, this habit of his seemed to be spreading to Bart, who in the past had always been a purposeful, down-to-business walker. On their epic journey to the office, he had spent four full minutes snuffling a patch of dirt at the base of a tree before ambling on. He hadn't even peed on it.

It had taken Maddie and the boys over half an hour to cover the same distance she normally travelled in about five minutes, leaving her with just enough time to accomplish exactly one task on her lengthy to-do list before her employees showed up for the day. As her walkers filtered in, Maddie set her work aside and sighed, resigning herself to an antisocial weekend of catching up.

Hannah was the third person through the door, and she looked fresh-faced and serene, completely unaware that any unpleasant experience was headed her way. She smiled easily and chatted with her coworkers and, when she saw Bart and Goliath, immediately proceeded to lavish them with attention, which the boys gladly accepted.

Maddie hated to break up the love fest, especially since Goliath was so blissful in the moment, something she was supposed to promote, not discourage. Maddie really didn't want to break Hannah's good mood either, certainly not first thing in the morning, but there was little time before she had to head out to meet Dottie. Before she could talk herself out of it, Maddie called Hannah over. She didn't have an office, per se, just a desk tucked in the corner, which was another reason she was seriously contemplating a move to expand the business. Maybe then she could have a private space with a door instead of taking employees outside for confidential conversations, which was easy enough in the summer, but the brutal Chicago winters made Maddie wish she could let employee indiscretions slide until the spring.

"Take a walk with me?" Maddie asked. Most of her employees knew that this request preceded a delicate conversation, one that required privacy, so they went willingly, though not eagerly. But even as she held the door open for Maddie, Hannah still seemed blithely unaware that trouble was headed her way. She tucked an errant lock of short brown hair behind her ear and smiled expectantly at Maddie, causing Maddie to hate her position just a little bit more.

She'd been the disciplinarian so infrequently that she still hadn't figured out the best approach—direct and to the point like ripping off a bandage? Or the agonizingly gentle façade of small talk and pleasantries before delivering criticism? She leaned toward the first approach and not just because of her time constraints that morning. Why pretend this was something that it wasn't? Maddie wasn't trying to befriend Hannah. She was trying to encourage better behavior.

"I wanted to touch base with you." Maddie hated the phrase "touch base," yet there it was, hanging in the air between them as they walked away from Little Guys. She couldn't seem to figure out how to get from touching base (and the mental flogging she delivered to herself for saying it) to where she wanted to be, so there was an uncomfortable silence—Hannah smiling, probably wondering what was wrong with her boss, while Maddie fumbled for words—until Maddie finally blurted out the problem. "I heard you were texting on your walks yesterday."

"Oh," Hannah replied as they rounded the corner. Her smile disappeared.

Maddie supposed that was better than tears or an impassioned denial, but she had little experience with resigned acceptance. It was weird, and she didn't know how to take it, so she just moved forward. "You know I don't allow that, right?"

"Yeah, you told me that."

Twice, Maddie could've said, if she'd felt like being a hard-ass, which she didn't.

"And you understand why it's not allowed? That it's not just me being difficult or controlling?"

"Yes, Miss Smithwick."

No one who worked for Maddie ever called her Miss Smithwick, and hearing it now made her feel like a mean teacher.

"Am I fired?" Hannah asked quietly.

"Not this time," Maddie answered, surprised by Hannah's directness. "But I won't have this conversation with you again. Understood?" They had doubled back and were again at Little Guys' front door.

Hannah nodded, refusing to make eye contact.

"Good." Maddie smiled sympathetically, but Hannah didn't see her boss's olive branch. Instead she skulked in the door, putting as much distance as possible between herself and Maddie.

Maddie hated being the cause of Hannah's somber mood, but she had no time to fret over it. She still had to confer with Patrick, distribute keys to her employees and then walk the boys home (in significantly less time than their earlier, lengthy commute, she hoped) before driving to the hospital.

"Sounds like you had a grotesquely full morning. I'm glad I slept through most of it," Dottie said as they reached Granny Doyle's room.

Granny was sitting up in bed, scowling at a forkful of scrambled eggs before putting it her mouth. The scowl deepened as she chewed. Maddie thought her grandmother looked more peaked than she had yesterday, but at least she was eating.

When Granny saw her visitors, her sour expression disappeared.

"Well, this is a treat." Granny Doyle beamed at the pair as they approached her bed. "What are you two doing here together?" She threw a little extra weight on the word "together" and smiled at Maddie, as if to say, "I told you so."

Granny's smile seemed genuine, and Maddie was pleased to see her grandmother looking so upbeat.

"We came to spring you, Mrs. Doyle." Dottie stooped down to give Granny a more enthusiastic hug and a kiss on the cheek than Granny was prepared for. "But we're still arguing about the plan."

"I appreciate the sentiment, but your timing is lousy, girls. These idiot doctors finally put their empty heads together and came up with one idea."

To her surprise, Maddie's chest tightened, and a knot formed in her stomach. She was glad to have news but terrified to learn it. "What's the diagnosis?"

"They think it's my blood pressure, but of course they aren't sure because that doesn't explain all of my symptoms. So they want to start experimenting with treatment options, of course. Running up my bill to pay for their mansions and sports cars, no doubt."

A wave of relief washed over Maddie as Granny griped about medical professionals. Blood pressure was practically nothing compared to the bleak diagnosis Maddie had built up in her head. With medication and, Maddie guessed, a few lifestyle changes, Granny would be fine.

"They claim they have to run a few more tests, including a stress test, but I told them not to waste their time. As long as I'm here, I already know that the answer to that one is yes," Granny cackled at her own joke. "Anyway, they started me on some pills this morning. If they work, I might be sprung in a day or two."

Maddie hugged her grandmother to her. "I'm so glad you're okay, Granny," she said, her voice trembling with emotion.

"Don't start crying on me, child. You sound like you were ready to plan my funeral."

"I told her that was nonsense, Mrs. Doyle, but Maddie refused to listen to reason."

Maddie wiped tears from her eyes and laughed, both from joy and at the idea of Dottie ever being the voice of reason.

"How did Goliath's appointment go?" Granny expertly changed the subject.

"Very well," Dottie practically purred. She had flipped the switch to come-hither mode, and she wasn't even the one hoping for a date with Dr. Sheridan.

Granny threw Maddie an inquiring glance, but Maddie ignored the implied question. "It was fine, Granny. I think he's doing better. He's started eating a little."

"That's good news."

"It is," Maddie agreed. "He seems to be getting better. Once I get the official word that he's healthy, I'm going to have to start looking for a new home for him."

Granny and Dottie both snorted at the same time.

"What? I can't have two dogs."

"Why not?"

"It costs a lot to feed two dogs, Granny."

"Not the way Goliath has been eating."

Having no patience for Dottie's input, Maddie glared at her friend. "I also don't have the time or the space."

"I don't see how it takes more time to care for two dogs instead of one. You walk them together, feed them together. Easy." Granny brushed her hands together in a gesture of finality. "And unless your house shrank since the last time I was there, you've got more than enough room for another dog."

"Anyway." Maddie decided the best way to handle the argument was to pretend it wasn't happening. She was sure Granny and Dottie would revisit the topic, but for now her plan was to ignore it. "The doctor is going to call me with his test results—"

"And an offer of matrimony," Dottie interjected.

"—but she thinks it's just depression." Maddie glossed over Dottie's interruption.

"You're going to have to back up a step, child. What's this about the doctor?"

Maddie's pointed glower at Dottie was cut short by her cell phone. Saved by the bell, she thought and then cringed at the latest entry in her string of clichés today. When she saw who was calling, she added one more to the list. "Speak of the devil," she muttered and then apologized to Granny and Dottie before answering.

"Miss Smithwick?" The sound of her own mispronounced name had never before been such a source of pleasure to Maddie.

"Hello Dr. Sheridan. Nadia," she corrected herself, remembering the doctor had invited Maddie to use her first name, then changed her mind again. "Dr. Sheridan." She was off to a great start in the sweet-talk department. Mortified, she turned her red face to the wall and took a hopefully calming breath. "Hello," he said and thought she heard Dr. Sheridan laughing on the other end of the line.

"I've got the results from Goliath's blood work, and everything is normal. He's a completely healthy, grief-stricken dog."

"That's a relief," Maddie said.

"Has he shown any improvement?"

Maddie told Dr. Sheridan about Goliath's gradually increased interest in food as well as his spurts of jubilation and activity, both with Bart and at the office. She hoped to impress the doctor by being a good dog guardian since beguiling her with language was out of the question. Maddie was rewarded with various "mmm-hmms" and "ahhs" of approval as she spoke, making Maddie wish she had more to report.

"Wonderful. I'm glad to hear he's doing better," the doctor said and advised Maddie to continue as she had been with Goliath. Maddie was so busy basking in Dr. Sheridan's faint praise that she almost missed the doctor's instruction to call if his condition didn't improve or worsened. Maddie began contemplating their future conversations, ostensibly centered on Goliath's health but with undertones of courtship. She was starting to believe that she might have a chance of hooking the doctor.

"Listen," Dr. Sheridan broke in on Maddie's reverie. "I've got such a full schedule today that I already know I'm going to be skipping lunch."

"Oh," Maddie said. Her body slumped in disappointment, and she steeled herself for the familiar, inevitable brush-off from Dr. Nadia Sheridan. "I understand."

"I'll be ravenous by the time I get out of here tonight," Dr. Sheridan continued. "I don't suppose you'd join me for dinner?"

"Wait," Maddie said, certain her hearing had failed her or that she had slipped back into fantasy. "Are you asking me out?"

"She'd love to," Dottie and Granny called out in unison loud enough to be heard at the nurses' station two floors up.

"Who's that?" Dr. Sheridan asked. She sounded both curious and amused.

"My grandmother and my former best friend." Maddie turned and glared. "They have issues with boundaries."

"That sounds frustrating," Dr. Sheridan said. "Unless of course they're telling you to say yes."

"They are."

"And is it working?"

"Yes. Their unnecessary encouragement has done the trick." Maddie turned away from Granny and Dottie's prying eyes. "I'd love to have dinner with you."

As Dr. Sheridan proposed a plan for the evening, Maddie could hear Granny and Dottie congratulating themselves, and she knew she would never hear the end of this. She didn't want to hang up and expose herself to their full torment, but Dr. Sheridan—Nadia—had to get back to her patients.

"Thank your grandmother and your friend for me," she said before she hung up and left Maddie defenseless.

Granny didn't even wait for Maddie to put her phone away. "So she's a doctor," she teased.

"Here we go," she muttered to herself, but even in the face of the relentless badgering she anticipated, Maddie couldn't stop smiling.

CHAPTER FIFTEEN

Maddie allowed Dottie and Granny to tease her for half an hour before she headed back to work. They poked fun at her awkwardness on the phone before they demanded the details of the date. Once Maddie revealed that Dr. Sheridan (whose first name she really ought to start using) would be taking her to Ella, a trendy restaurant in Lincoln Park, Dottie launched into an all-out assault on Maddie's wardrobe, much to Granny's delight. Dottie riffed for a full fifteen minutes, forbidding Maddie from wearing shorts, pants, a T-shirt, anything with pockets or "one of those gunny sacks you call a dress" and then detailed what items in Maddie's wardrobe would be acceptable for a first date at an upscale dining establishment. It was a short list.

Even though Dottie's unsolicited (but not wholly unwelcome) advice stung, Maddie endured it because Granny was enjoying it so much. She laughed and smiled more in that brief span of time than she had in the past four days combined. How could Maddie deny her so much obvious joy? Maddie also knew that Granny and Dottie's taunting was their unconventional way of showing their love, not that she wouldn't have preferred a hug. Nevertheless, she had to get back to work, so she needed to end their fun eventually, and when she said goodbye, even after all their teasing, Maddie's good mood remained intact.

After leaving the hospital, she headed directly to her first walk of the day, and though she had felt flustered and rushed before visiting Granny, like she would never have enough time to finish everything she needed to do, she now felt at ease. Rather than stressing over what was next and how she would get all of her work done, she savored each appointment with her clients, cheerfully tending to each dog's specific and sometimes odd needs.

Her delight bubbled over as she told every dog in her care about the improvements in her love life and her grandmother's health. Although they probably didn't understand the importance of these developments, they still gazed at her in joyful recognition of her good news, which helped her hang on to her joyful composure as she faced the peculiarities of her day. She smiled as she carried all thirty-five pounds of Munchkin Stavros—thirteen years old and arthritic—down three flights of stairs, and she waited patiently as Bear Curtis, a notorious lingerer, pawed delicately at the grass just outside his door for ten minutes before he even entertained the notion of peeing. She found the scavenging antics of the aptly named Bandit Jarvis amusing rather than frustrating, and not even Dolly Alvarado, a St. Bernard-Lab mix who had, on occasion, pulled so hard that she'd lifted Maddie off the ground, could destroy Maddie's bliss.

Back at the office after her final walk (an easy, uneventful stroll with Harvey Baxter), Maddie crossed another item off her to-do list, fielded a few phone calls (none of which came from her mysterious harasser) and even managed to contact the human members of the Whelan-Silver household to set up her first investigative sting operation. The conversation had gone better than she'd expected, and Adam and Albert had agreed to meet her the next day to discuss her services and, unbeknownst to them, their possible involvement in Howard's death. She even had a quiet minute to herself before her walkers returned to headquarters to hand in their keys and wrap up the week. All in all, Maddie felt satisfied and productive, chipper even, when she wished Patrick a good weekend and headed home for the day.

At home, faced with the prospect of getting ready to go out (instead of her usual internal debate over whether the rewards of cooking for one justified the hassle of cleanup) panic set in. In a vain attempt to settle her nerves, Maddie spent forty-five minutes playing in the yard with the boys before feeding them. Then she sat for twenty minutes, staring at her clothes, waiting for some kind of inspiration, as a feeling of dread began to weigh her down. Before it overtook her completely, Maddie called the only person who could keep her from panicking and cancelling on Dr. Sheridan.

"How fast can you get here?"

"Matilda? Shouldn't you be getting ready for your date?"

"Why do you think I'm calling, Dottie? I don't know what I'm doing."

"Precious, if you don't know how to be a lesbian by now, I don't know what you think I can do to help you."

"Dottie, please be serious, just this once." Maddie felt herself on the verge of tears. "I need your help."

"I've got a date of my own to prepare for, hon."

"I don't know what I'm doing, Dottie." Certain she couldn't handle this alone, Maddie broke down. "I have no idea what to wear or how to act or why I'm even doing this. I need you. Please, Dottie," she begged, "please help me."

Dottie let out a long, slow breath before speaking. "I'll be there in twenty minutes. Get yourself cleaned up. I want a blank canvas to work with."

The relief Maddie felt at the sound of those words was almost unsettling. When had dressing herself for a date become such an insurmountable task? How had she let herself become such a hermit that the thought of grooming herself for social interaction was crippling? Hopeful that tonight signified an end to the recent antisocial phase of her life, Maddie headed to the bathroom, followed by Bart and Goliath. As she stepped over the dogs and into the shower, her thoughts turned from her social inadequacies to wondering just how blank Dottie wanted her "canvas" to be.

"I'm sure she'll hyperventilate if I don't remove all the hair I can live without," Maddie told the boys and then reached for her razor.

Even after the most meticulous bathing and cautious shaving of her life, Maddie had still only managed to spend fifteen minutes in the shower. She calculated that she'd have another half an hour to wait for her habitually tardy friend. On the upside, she had managed to remove all of her leg hair and none of the skin for maybe the third time since she'd started shaving almost twenty years ago. Usually she accomplished the seemingly impossible task of leaving tufts of hair jutting out of skinless patches of her legs. This was a refreshing change.

Maddie was still contemplating the benefits of careful grooming when Dottie strode through her bedroom door (fifteen minutes later than she said she'd arrive, which was ten minutes earlier than Maddie expected her) and produced a dress from a garment bag.

"Put this on, pet, and thank me tomorrow."

"This is beautiful, Dottie." Maddie didn't recognize the sleeveless black knit dress. "But if it's one of yours, I'll look like a clown in it—a delusional, flat-chested clown."

"I wouldn't dream of putting you in one of my gowns, sweets. It's yours."

Maddie stared at Dottie. Knowing the kinds of places Dottie shopped, Maddie suspected the price tag would reveal an amount higher than her mortgage payment. "Dottie, I can't—"

"Nonsense, love. Consider it an early birthday present."

"My birthday is in March."

"I said 'early.'"

"Thank you, Dottie." On the verge of tears again, Maddie hugged her friend.

"There's no time to cry, doll face. Get yourself dressed while I contemplate the rest of your look."

As she dressed, Maddie tried to calm her nerves by talking about anything but the date. What was a better distraction than murder? "I'm meeting with Adam and Albert tomorrow."

"How did you arrange that?" Dottie fastened the dress and began to tackle Maddie's hair.

Maddie never had the patience to dry and style her hair, which is why it usually ended up in a ponytail or a braid, but Dottie seemed to enjoy the effort of taming Maddie's normally unruly curls into soft waves.

"I offered them a free trial week of walks."

"Smart work, cookie."

"I thought so." Maddie smiled, pleased with her ingenuity. "While we're discussing the details, I'm going to try to get answers to some of my questions."

"I hope you're planning to be more tactful in your approach than you were last time. You don't want to spook them."

"I promise I'll behave. I want to get an idea of their schedules. If neither of them had the opportunity to be at Howard's house the morning he was killed, then I won't need to press further. If they did, though, I have to try to get them talking about Howard."

"Good luck, sunshine." Dottie stepped back and eyed Maddie critically. "Go have a look," Dottie said and steered Maddie to her full-length mirror.

If she had Dottie on hand every day, Maddie thought, she might look presentable more often. The dress had a sort of twirly, flared skirt that ended above the knee, showing off her legs, which were arguably her best feature. The sheer upper portion that turned what would otherwise be a strapless dress into more of an elegant tank top brought on a fresh wave of anxiety—she wasn't used to being so exposed—but the dress was otherwise perfect.

"You don't think it's a little too revealing?" Maddie gestured to the gauzy fabric that barely covered her chest. "I feel like I'm on display."

"Niblet, I know you better than anyone, and I know you won't be assertive on this date. No, you'll be too busy questioning the reality of it." Maddie would have protested, but what would be the point? Dottie was right. Sometimes she hated that Dottie knew her so well. "That means you have to inspire the doctor to be assertive. This dress is very inspirational." Dottie made a few slight adjustments as she spoke. "Just one more thing."

Dottie left the room for a moment and returned with a shoebox. "I know the only footwear I'll find in your closet is running shoes—thousands of running shoes, as if you can use more than one pair at a time—so I got you these."

Maddie felt certain that the shoes Dottie held before her were designed by a leading expert in torture. Or a stilts manufacturer.

"Heels? You want me to wear heels?"

"You have a problem with elegant footwear? Never mind. I already know the answer to that question."

"Do you remember the last time you made me wear heels? At your second wedding?"

"The best man was six and a half feet tall. Standing next to him you would have looked like you were on an excursion from Munchkinland."

"Which would have been so much worse than when I lost my balance and ended up giving the mother of the groom a lap dance. Heels and I do not agree."

"I'm not asking you to join Cirque du Soleil. You just have to get from the house to the car, the car to the restaurant and back without falling. An infant could do it."

"I'm trying to impress this woman. In a good way."

"Don't be so fatalistic, Matilda. It's two tiny inches that will make your gorgeous legs even gorgeouser. Trust me."

"Is there even the slightest possibility that you're going to give in?"

Hands on her hips, Dottie said, "Do you really need to ask?"

Shaking her head and muttering under her breath, Maddie wedged her poor feet (accustomed to roomy, comfortable, cushioned shoes) into the offensive footwear. She stole a glance at the mirror and decided not to tell Dottie, who was already beaming with self-satisfaction, that she was right.

"I have outdone myself. You are perfection, pigeon. Your date is going to lose the power of speech when she sees you. What time is she picking you up?"

"She's not picking me up. We're meeting there."

Dottie blinked for several moments in stupefied silence. Then the dam broke. "You're meeting there? Like this is some kind of inconsequential blind date? Like you're in junior high and need a ride from your parents? Or worse, like you're not worthy of being escorted to your destination?"

"Like she has to work, and we won't get to eat until midnight if I insist on being carted around like a princess."

"Fine, but I am not sending you off in that coif-wrecking vehicle you insist upon driving." Dottie folded her arms across her chest in resignation.

"You'd prefer I take a bus?"

"Heavens no! You might as well show up in a burlap sack. I'll drive you myself, but we have to go now." Dottie headed toward the door, but Maddie, terrified, couldn't make herself move.

"What if she doesn't like me?" she asked in a small voice.

"Don't be silly, chicklet. She already likes you. That's why she's opting to spend her leisure time with you. In a chic, expensive restaurant where it's next to impossible to secure a reservation, I might add. She's gone to a lot of trouble if she's not interested."

"You're right," Maddie said. After this night was over, she would have to do something special to thank Dottie for repeatedly coming to her rescue.

"There's no need to be nervous. It's only dinner, not a lifelong commitment. I know that violates the lesbian code of conduct, but you don't need to get engaged tonight."

"Says the woman who's been married three times."

Dottie ignored Maddie's comment. "Just be yourself and have fun. Get back in the saddle, or however you ladies do things."

Maddie barely had time to roll her eyes before her more sure-footed friend whisked her out the door.

CHAPTER SIXTEEN

The restaurant, nestled within the dense foliage of Lincoln Park, was nicer than any Maddie had been to in a very long time, possibly since her last first date, which had taken place a depressing four years ago (however, this probably wasn't the best time to think about that). Maddie noted with pleasure the spacious layout of the dining room. Though the owners could have crammed at least a dozen more tables into the space (the cost of which had to be astronomical), they'd opted for fewer tables with more space between them. Not only did it provide room for the waitstaff to maneuver through the dining room with ease, but it also created an air of privacy which Maddie appreciated. She hated feeling like she had to whisper loud enough so that her companion could hear but soft enough so that the stranger at her elbow didn't drink in her every word. Nor did she want to eavesdrop by default on her fellow diners.

The décor was minimal, mostly relying on the architecture of the building to create a classic, simple feel that was at once open and inviting. Framed black and white photographs hung here and there on the three exposed-brick walls of the dining room. The images, all of the city, taken by someone who knew and loved it, were for sale, but one quick glance at the price of the piece Maddie liked best told her she wouldn't be adding it to her collection any time soon. The fourth wall, on the east side of the dining room, was actually a series of glass doors that led to a patio with a view of the Lincoln Park Lagoon. Maddie imagined that in the daytime, or on a clearer night, the scene would be breathtaking.

After a cursory review of the menu, she understood how the proprietors could survive in this location. She saw nothing, not even appetizers, for under forty dollars. That should have settled her nerves a bit—Maddie doubted that Dr. Sheridan would spend so lavishly if she wasn't serious about this date—but it didn't help at all. Maddie took a calming sip of her martini and, noting its strength, decided to take it easy. She wasn't driving, but she also didn't want to turn this into her last date with Dr. Sheridan.

Finally deciding on the wild mushroom risotto—with no sauces to splash on herself or bad-breath inducing ingredients—as the safest choice for a date, Maddie glanced up from her menu to see Nadia watching her, wearing that crooked smile that Maddie had been so smitten with the day before. It hadn't lost any of its impact since its debut. In fact, Nadia looked even better than Maddie remembered. Part of that might be the change in wardrobe—she'd traded in her scrubs for a white sleeveless blouse and black slacks that seemed tailor-made for her curves. On top of that, Nadia also opted to wear her hair down, letting it fall in loose waves around her face. She looked like she just stepped out of a shampoo ad, and Maddie resisted the urge to run her fingers through Nadia's hair. Instead, she smiled back.

"You saved me from a night of Hot Pockets and channel surfing," Nadia said. "Thank you."

"You're assuming I'm the better option. Hot Pockets are delicious."

"But you're far better looking, so I have high hopes."

Maddie felt herself blush and looked away, hoping to conceal the splotchy evidence of her embarrassment. She decided to steer the conversation away from her appearance by asking the question that had been nagging at her since she spoke with Nadia that morning. "I'm wondering, is this—us being here together—is it…legal?"

"Some places might still frown on it, but I think we're in the clear in a liberal town like Chicago."

Maddie laughed, at herself as much as at Nadia's gentle teasing. "No, I mean, isn't there some policy against dating your clients?"

"Absolutely. I'm strict about that. Can you imagine the potential turmoil otherwise?"

"If dating clients isn't allowed, how are you on a date with a client?"

Nadia's smirk—like she knew a secret and wasn't sure she would be sharing it—brought on a fresh wave of anxiety for Maddie. What if she'd optimistically misread all of the signs? What if this wasn't really a date? Though it certainly seemed like one, or at least what Maddie remembered dates being like. If Nadia looked that good when she wasn't on a date, how on earth was she still single?

"Well," Nadia broke in on Maddie's panicked mental ramblings. "You're not my client. You go to Dr. Mitra." Nadia winked and smiled. "By the way, I have never been more thrilled not to take on a new client."

Pleased and relieved, Maddie relaxed a little.

"We're not completely off the hook, though."

Maddie instantly regretted letting her guard down and asked what the problem was.

"Franklin would be very upset if he knew I was here with you."

At a complete loss, Maddie asked, "Who is Franklin?"

"You met him yesterday. You left quite an impression on him."

Maddie reflected on the previous day but couldn't remember meeting anyone other than Howard's nosy neighbor. While he might enjoy sharing the details of Maddie and Nadia's night out (strictly from a gossip standpoint), she doubted he'd be upset by it. Anyway, his name was Lester, not Franklin. Suddenly, it hit her. "The nervous vet tech?" Nadia nodded. "He doesn't agree with the Dr. Mitra loophole?" Maddie asked.

"If he knew about it, he'd not only agree with it. He'd want to take advantage of it himself."

"Excuse me?" Maddie asked before taking another sip of her drink.

"He said you're the most beautiful woman he's ever seen."

Maddie choked on her martini but refrained from spitting it across the table. "He works with *you*, and he thinks that *I'm* the most beautiful woman he's ever seen? I think Franklin needs to see an optometrist."

"He's my nephew, so I'm pretty sure both of our heads would explode if he ever thought of me as being in any way attractive. Besides, he's right."

Maddie felt her face get hot, and she squirmed a little under Nadia's intense gaze.

"You don't take compliments well, do you?"

"I'm just not used to them, unless they're about top grades, hard work or general good behavior."

"I'll have to see what I can do to change that." Nadia smiled again.

When the waiter appeared to take their orders, Nadia's attention was diverted. When he left, Maddie changed the subject.

"Why did you become a vet?"

"It's a long story."

"I'm not going anywhere."

"It's really not that interesting."

"My best friend, Dottie, has dragged me to more than one cosmetics trend show. Believe me, I can handle long and boring, but if your story ends in me getting a makeover, we're going to have a problem."

Despite her apparent reluctance, Nadia delved into the story anyway. "I grew up in a tiny town in the middle of nowhere. No one outside of town has ever heard of it, and almost anyone who's ever left wants to forget about it immediately."

"What was so awful about it?"

"Among other things, the people in town weren't what you would call open-minded, so they didn't exactly welcome my family to the community."

Maddie was about to ask for an explanation, but Nadia anticipated her question.

"My dad is white, but my mom isn't. Even though I had a 'normal' last name, I didn't look like the other kids. As if that wasn't bad enough, on the rare occasion that I could get any schoolmates to come to my house, my mom always insisted on feeding them."

"Isn't that a good thing?" Several of Maddie's early friendships had been solidified by the addition of Granny Doyle's oatmeal cookies.

"If she'd made regular food, yes. But she was the town's self-appointed multiculturalism committee of one. As if she could win over an eight-year-old with steamed fish and dal bhat. She just made everything worse."

Maddie's heart broke to think of the loneliness Nadia must have faced. She couldn't imagine treating someone as a pariah just because of her heritage, but she had grown up in one of the most culturally diverse neighborhoods in Chicago. Her childhood friends had been a mini United Nations.

"Then, on top of being the weird half foreign kid, in high school I figured out that I was gay, and that just gave the kids another reason to avoid me. Needless to say, I didn't do much socializing, but I wasn't alone." Nadia grinned, obviously approaching a less painful part of her story. "I was forever bringing home animals—dogs, cats, birds, even a goat once. My parents found a home for the goat, but they let me keep everyone else. I think they knew how lonely I was, and the animals kept me company. They were my friends, and I knew I would be happiest working with animals." Nadia smiled again. "I'm also kind of bossy, so I knew I would have to be the one in charge. Veterinary medicine just made sense."

"What horrible people. No wonder you don't want to look back. I'm so sorry"

"Don't be. I love my job, and if even one of those little bigots had been nice to me, I might not have taken this path. In a way, I should be thanking them."

"You are incredible." Their food arrived, and Maddie beamed at Nadia while the waiter tended to them. "I can't imagine feeling anything but hatred for every single one of them."

"Don't give me so much credit. I also often imagine all of them dying of a hideous wasting disease."

"Seems fair," Maddie said.

Their conversation continued as they ate, sharing bites of one another's food, which was well worth the price. By the time dessert arrived, they had completed the obligatory discussion of exes and family, which of course included pets. Maddie's heart broke again when Nadia spoke of her dog, Maude, who had died just before Christmas. She longed for another pet but didn't think it would be fair to the animal, given her current hectic schedule. Maddie also learned that Nadia had one sibling, a sister named Meredith who was eleven years older and had left home as soon as she turned eighteen. They obviously hadn't been close growing up but had developed a better relationship over the years. Still, they saw each other only once or twice a year. Maddie couldn't fathom being that distant from her sisters and once again reflected on the loneliness of Dr. Sheridan's life.

As the night progressed, a light rain started falling, but they were so focused on each other that neither woman noticed the change in the weather until they stepped outside. In part Maddie looked forward to the all-out downpour promised by the thunder rumbling overhead—assuming it would offer a reprieve from the high temperatures rather than plunging them into even more intolerable heat and humidity—but the part of her that would have to combine grace and speed as she ran through a near-monsoon in her Dottie-imposed footwear hoped that the storm would hold off until Nadia dropped her off at home.

Her luck held out, at least until she got into Nadia's car, an electric blue Mini that was in stark contrast to the impressions of Nadia that Maddie had collected throughout dinner. She had expected Nadia to drive something more utilitarian and basic. She found this choice surprising, which she apparently let slip as Nadia headed toward Lake Shore Drive.

"This is a nice car."

"You sound surprised. Were you expecting me to drive a beater?" Nadia laughed.

"I was thinking of something more in the SUV family, actually."

"That's weirdly perceptive of you. I used to have a Cherokee, and I still miss her." Nadia sounded wistful. "Sorry. I've only had this car for three weeks, and we haven't bonded yet."

"What made you pick a Mini?"

Traffic crawled to a stop as the rain grew heavier, and though Nadia was alert and cautious, she didn't seem stressed by the conditions. "I didn't. It was actually a gift from Howard."

Maddie was stunned. She knew Howard had been a generous man, but this seemed a little extreme. What could Nadia possibly have done for Howard to inspire the extravagant gift of a car? A gift card to Target was one thing, but a brand new car? And this was no stripped-down, bare-bones, plain but functional vehicle. It was a great car to begin with, and it appeared as if Howard had sprung for more than a few optional bells and whistles. How could Nadia have accepted it? Since it didn't seem wise to ask any of these questions, Maddie settled for a flip comment. "I guess you're an even better vet than I realized."

Nadia laughed again. "I helped him with a project, and he wanted to thank me. I told him it wasn't necessary. I had a perfectly good car, so I refused."

The wall of vehicles in front of them began moving again, and Nadia inched forward.

"What happened to change your mind?"

"My car was stolen. When the police found it, it had been torched, and the settlement my insurance company offered wouldn't have covered bus fare for a month. Howard's generous offer became too good to pass up, but I insisted on making payments. He didn't like that, but it was the only way I could live with myself."

A feeling of relief washed over Maddie. She hadn't liked thinking of Nadia as a mercenary person and preferred knowing that their values were much more in alignment than that. Curious, Maddie asked, "What was the project?"

"He wanted to breed Goliath. I helped."

Maddie was starting to get whiplash from her alternating opinions of Nadia. The idea that a vet, a professed lover of animals, had helped to increase the pet population when there were already so many dogs in need of loving homes, floored Maddie. "How much help did you give him?" She couldn't keep the brittle edge out of her voice.

"I helped him get his paperwork in order. I connected him with some suitable dams, and I examined all of the dogs, those I found as well as those he located on his own, before the event. If any weren't a good match, I let Howard know."

"And it didn't bother you that you were adding to the pet population when there are already thousands of dogs in desperate need of homes?"

"It bothered me greatly, which is why I tried to discourage Howard, but he insisted on going forward no matter what. I decided that it would be better for all of the animals involved if I didn't let him learn what to do through trial and error. I also made him promise that each of the puppies would have a home, even if that meant *his* home, and I got him to make a sizable donation to The Anti-Cruelty Society. I did what I could to make the situation better."

"Oh." Maddie stared at her hands in her lap. She really needed to think before speaking. "I'm sorry."

"If there's one thing you never have to apologize to me for, it's concern over the welfare of animals." Nadia reached over to give Maddie's hand a reassuring squeeze. Their fingers entwined, and they continued holding hands until Nadia parked down the street from Maddie's house.

"Would you like to come in?" Maddie asked. She wasn't ready for the evening to end, especially so soon after her rudeness. "You can wait out the storm, and I know Goliath would love to see you."

"Is he the only one who'd be happy about it?"

"No." Maddie shook her head and kissed Nadia's hand. "Come inside."

Inside, as the dogs circled them and barked with excitement, Maddie realized the impression she must have given Nadia. Maddie wondered what Nadia would be expecting, and she felt a nervous fluttering in her stomach.

"Can I get you something to drink?"

"What have you got?" Nadia followed Maddie into the kitchen, the dogs trailing behind them.

"Just about everything. Being Dottie's best friend means I'm contractually obligated to keep a fully stocked bar." Maddie laughed anxiously as her date stepped closer to her, so close they were practically touching. Maddie could smell Nadia's perfume. It was a clean, delicate, almost fruity scent that made Maddie weak-kneed and fuzzy-headed. "Or if you'd prefer, I have coffee or tea."

"I can skip the drink," Nadia said, before her lips, at once soft and powerful, took hungry possession of Maddie's. Maddie felt herself melting into the embrace, opening herself to Nadia, and then a familiar, tantalizing heat filled her body as their kiss deepened. Maddie's hands were in Nadia's hair, pulling her closer. Her head swam, and she moaned as Nadia's hands travelled lightly up her arms. She felt a stirring of desire when Nadia's hand reached her breast, and moaning again, she broke the kiss.

"Wow." Maddie released her hold on Nadia's hair and rested her hands on Nadia's strong shoulders.

"Wow indeed." Nadia moved to kiss Maddie again, but Maddie stopped her.

"Something wrong?" Nadia's heavy-lidded eyes were focused on Maddie's mouth, and her hand, which she hadn't removed from Maddie's breast, seemed to be moving of its own accord, lightly caressing and stirring further desire.

"I'm not ready for this to go where it seems like it's going."

"Really?" Nadia arched an eyebrow as she shifted her glance from Maddie's face to the hand that covered Maddie's breast, which offered undeniable evidence of Maddie's arousal.

Damn her turncoat body. "Okay, so my body is ready. It's so ready it's considering mutiny right now. But I need more time."

Nadia stepped back and dropped her hands to her sides.

"I've been single for a long time," Maddie explained, "and it would be easy for me to rush into something. I want to be sure I'm rushing for the right reasons. Not because I'm lonely but because you are an incredible, intelligent, beautiful woman who makes me a little delirious in very good ways."

Though she nodded, Nadia's expression was unreadable.

"I hope that I'm not driving you away by telling you this, that there will be more swoon-worthy dates in our future." Maddie stepped closer to Nadia, terrified to continue but needing to be clear. She took Nadia's hand and kissed her softly. "I want something that's worth waiting for. Does that make sense?"

"It does. It absolutely does." Nadia dropped Maddie's hand and reached for her keys.

"You don't have to leave."

"If I stay, I'll try to change your mind." Nadia smiled, though it didn't reach her eyes.

Maddie felt desperate to end the night on a hopeful note. "What are your plans for tomorrow?" she asked.

"I have to work." Nadia sounded dejected, like someone had taken her favorite toy from her. "What are you up to tomorrow?"

"I'm meeting some potential clients. I'm mostly seeing them so I can figure out if either of them had anything to do with Howard's murder. Hopefully they're both innocent and I'm subtle enough that I don't upset them. I really would like them as clients." Maddie knew she was rambling.

Nadia's face registered her concern. "You're investigating Howard's death? Is that wise?"

"Probably not, but I have to."

"Don't you think the police should handle this?"

"They are, most likely better than I am, but I need to know for me. Someone murdered my friend, hurt Goliath in the process and might be spreading the rumor that I did it. I can't just stand by and do nothing. I have to clear my name, and I have to know who could be so cruel to such a sweet man." Maddie was worked up, fevered with anger and sadness.

Nadia drew Maddie to her and held her close until she calmed down. She kissed Maddie's forehead and said, "Just be careful, okay?"

"I promise."

Nadia kissed her again and smiled. "But you're free tomorrow night?"

"I am."

"I'll call you tomorrow." She kissed Maddie's cheek and whispered, "I want something worth waiting for too."

CHAPTER SEVENTEEN

The dogs let Maddie sleep until seven and, feeling rested and cheerful upon waking, Maddie thought a special outing was in order. She called the boys to her and asked if they wanted to go to the beach. Bart, who would have gone to the beach three hundred sixty-five days a year if given the opportunity, danced in a little circle and barked. Then, as he raced to the door and back to Maddie, urging her to move faster, his toenails clicked on the floor, reminding her that he was overdue for a spa day. Goliath, swept up by Bart's infectious mood, added his deep bark to the joyous cacophony as he loped to the door where Bart now stood, his entire body propelled by his wagging tail. Maddie grabbed their leashes and followed them out the door.

With all the fun of playing with other dogs, romping in the sand and frolicking in the water, the beach offered endless entertainment for Bart, and since it was just four blocks from Maddie's house, she brought him as often as she could. Dogs technically weren't allowed on the beach. They were supposed to go to one of the designated dog beaches farther south, but those were often crowded and dirty and not worth the time spent driving there or the hassle of parking. Early in the morning, the beach at the end of her street was empty by comparison, almost like a private beach. And since the lifeguards didn't show up until nine, as long as Maddie and the other dog owners cleared out by then, there were usually no complaints about Rogers Park's unofficial dog beach.

Their walk was brisk but pleasant. The rain the night before had offered welcome relief from the heat—Maddie guessed that the temperature had dropped by at least ten degrees. It would be even cooler by the lake, but the humidity hadn't changed. That, and the gray clouds obstructing the sun, indicated that they were in for more rain in the coming days. For now, though, the day was almost perfect, and she planned to let the dogs enjoy it as much as possible.

As soon as their feet hit the sand, Maddie let Bart off his leash, adding another broken law to her growing list of transgressions that morning. He raced to join his best dog friends Simon, Ozzy and Lily as they romped in and out of the water. Though Goliath showed interest in the dog festivities before him, Maddie didn't dare let him off leash. She didn't trust him to come when called, nor did she relish the idea of chasing him all over the beach when it was time to go. For now, he'd have to settle for more restrained fun. So while Bart dashed in and out of the water chasing or being chased by his dog friends, Goliath hopped around, eager to romp with the other animals but limited in his play by being tethered to Maddie, not that she offered much resistance. When excitement overtook him, she bobbed along behind him like a flightless kite.

The usual collection of dog owners milled about, some conversing, others throwing balls into the lake in an effort to wear out their furry bundles of energy. Most people commented on Goliath's appearance, impressed by his handsome bearing. When asked if she'd gotten a new dog, Maddie shared Goliath's story (without going into the gory specifics) and requested help finding him a permanent home. No one volunteered to take him in, but they all promised to let Maddie know if they found anyone who would. If anyone could be trusted to find a suitable forever family for Goliath, it was the group of dog lovers who stood before her, and Maddie felt better knowing she had their support.

Maddie let Bart play for an hour. In that time he'd managed to become a sopping-wet, sand-caked mess, but he was overjoyed. Goliath, though he hadn't enjoyed the freedom that Bart had, also seemed to be in a good mood. As they walked home, both dogs glanced back at her with love and happiness in their eyes. Their obvious satisfaction pleased Maddie. She loved humoring the boys, especially since the rest of the day would be so boring for them while she focused on work.

Once home, she spent the better part of four hours catching up on the tasks she'd neglected since Howard's death. Bart, exhausted from his morning activities, slept soundly on his bed, but Goliath, who hadn't worked off nearly as much energy, interrupted Maddie's progress from time to time with his whining requests for attention. A welcome distraction from the business before her, meeting his demands with a quick game of tug or fetch in the yard called her attention to his improved mood, which naturally turned her thoughts to Nadia. She'd been trying not to dwell on memories of their date, but since it was the best night she'd had in a very long time, she couldn't help herself. Intermittently, thoughts of her momentary rudeness and the less than satisfying end to the evening cast a shadow over her good mood, but she reminded herself that Nadia had said she'd call. Maddie had no idea when the call would come, but the promise of a second date wiped away her fleeting gloom.

By noon, she'd accomplished enough that she decided to take a break, possibly until Monday. She'd wiped out most of her to-do list, and even with her breaks for fun with Goliath, her eyes and back hurt from so much time in front of the computer. She did not envy people whose jobs required them to be chained to a desk and computer for eight hours a day. Even in the heart of the Polar Vortex—when the brutal temperatures and harsh wind chill had rendered even the most painstaking bundling up pointless—she was certain she'd still prefer to be moving around outside.

She had an hour before her meeting with Adam and Albert, and she still wasn't sure what she would say to them to get them talking about Howard. Traditionally, she didn't excel at impromptu speech. She liked to plan ahead whenever possible, but inspiration failed her in this instance. She was going to have to wing it, a prospect that didn't ease her anxiety in the least, so she busied herself with other tasks, like tidying her already clean house, to distract herself.

She waited until twenty minutes before she had to leave to check in with her grandmother. While Maddie wanted to know how Granny's new medicine was working, she also wanted to avoid any discussion about her date. For now, she wanted to have that all to herself, so she put off the call to her grandmother (and her inevitable conversation with Dottie) as long as possible, hoping they'd run out of time to talk before Granny got a chance to ask about the date. They didn't.

After answering Maddie's opening question about her health with a snappy "I'm fine," Granny immediately inquired about Maddie's evening.

"It was fine," Maddie replied, following her grandmother's lead. "Is the medicine working?"

"So far, so good," Granny answered. "Tell me about the restaurant. Was it nice?"

And so their battle of conversational wills began. It raged on for several minutes, neither woman willing to concede victory and discuss her own issue, until Granny forced her granddaughter to cooperate. "Your mom and dad are here," she announced, "and they want to know about your date too."

Great. If her parents knew, then her sisters would know before long (if they didn't already), which meant she was in for more teasing. And they wondered why she didn't socialize much.

"I'm glad there's nothing more important going on in the world." Maddie knew she sounded irritated. She hated being short with her grandmother. On top of making her seem like an ingrate, it also put her in line for a much-deserved reprimand.

"Now, don't get bent out of shape, child. We're interested because we care about you and we want you to be happy. And because the only other thing anybody wants to talk about is my health, which is not up for discussion."

Properly admonished, Maddie gave her grandmother what she wanted. "Tell everyone that it went well." Maddie shared some minor details to appease Granny. Though she left out the part about the spine-melting kiss, she did mention that Nadia would be calling later that day.

"Now that wasn't so hard, was it?" Granny asked.

"It was almost as easy as getting you to talk about your health," Maddie teased.

Though she could be maddening, Granny always meant well. As Maddie headed to her appointment, she decided that her grandmother's increased obstinacy meant that she must be feeling better. She would have preferred to confirm Granny's improvement with someone in the know, but that would have to wait until after her meeting when she intended to call her mother.

Maddie pulled up in front of Adam and Albert's house ten minutes before she was due. Pleased with her punctuality, she studied their home, as if the exterior of a house could be an accurate indicator of someone's capacity for murder. They lived in a gorgeous Victorian home in Evanston, technically outside her service area, though not by much. She was willing to commute a little farther because, as she told Nadia, she wanted to eliminate Adam and Albert as suspects. She also hoped that, if they were innocent, these dog-loving men would make excellent clients.

The pale blue exterior of their house looked freshly painted, and the sprawling, well-tended lawn was a lush, vibrant green. They hadn't added any personalized decorative touches to the outside—no flags (American or pride), no political signs and, not surprisingly, nothing cutsie like lawn geese or garden statuary. They didn't even have a birdbath. The property reminded Maddie of the cover of an architecture or design magazine rather than the home of potential clients and possible murderers. But, as she knew from her college days, that same historical charm was common to many homes in Evanston.

The men greeted Maddie cordially and ushered her through their pristine and well-furnished home (as impressive inside as out) to the back patio where Alphonse waited patiently for them. As usual when she met a dog, Maddie held out her closed hand for the dog to sniff, and when he indicated his acceptance of her, she gently stroked the fur on his neck and shoulders. Gradually she worked her way to his head, scratching behind his ears and under his chin before turning her attention back to his dads.

"What a beautiful boy, and he's so well behaved," she said, and both men beamed at her praise.

Adam and Albert had set out iced tea and snacks at a glass-topped table, and they invited Maddie to sit. Alphonse followed her to her seat, and he leaned in for some petting as she got down to business. She reiterated her offer of free walks, then asked, "Would I be walking Alphonse at the same time every day, or do you have flexibility in your schedules that would affect my visits?"

"That's a great question," Albert said. His voice was deep and rich, perfect for public speaking. The well-formed muscles in his tanned arms drew Maddie's attention as he poured her a drink and offered her something to eat. She began to appreciate Dottie's glowing assessment of him. "My schedule is beastly."

"He works all the time," Adam jumped in. He smiled proudly at his partner. "Leaves home at six in the morning, works twelve-hour days, minimum, and he even goes in on the weekends."

"That sounds brutal," Maddie admitted. "Don't you ever take a break during the day?"

"I take breathers here and there to decompress." Albert grinned. "I like to approach all of my deals with a fresh mind."

"Do you ever come home for one of your breathers?"

"There's no time for that. My office is in the Loop. All of my deals are downtown, and I only give myself fifteen or twenty minute breaks. Usually, the best I can do is grab another cup of coffee."

"That makes sense." Relieved, Maddie thought that Albert couldn't possibly have killed Howard, unless he was lying about his schedule. "What about you, Adam? What do your days look like?"

"That's where things get tricky."

Uh-oh. Maddie sipped her tea, waiting for his explanation.

"I'm a teacher, so I have a lot of free time in the summer. I try to keep myself busy around the house and with gardening."

Maddie surveyed the backyard. Aside from the mowed lawn and a large patch of dirt along the fence line, there was no evidence that anyone had done anything that could be called gardening.

He followed her glance and laughed. "I'm a lousy gardener," he said. "I actually started taking gardening classes last week. I hope I can keep at least one plant alive through the summer." He laughed again.

Maddie chuckled politely. "When is your class?"

"Monday and Wednesday mornings from ten to noon."

Howard died on a Tuesday morning, so Adam still wasn't off the hook.

"Are you home the rest of the time?" Maddie prayed that he had some rigid, very public activity that occupied his Tuesday mornings, something that offered him an irrefutable alibi.

"Pretty much," he answered, filling Maddie with an odd mixture of disappointment that he could be guilty and excitement that her sleuthing might actually bear some fruit. He explained how he filled his days—running errands, tending to Alphonse and caring for their home. There was nothing that eliminated him as a suspect or, for that matter, necessitated her services. She asked why they wanted a dog walker.

"His last walker didn't work out," Adam offered cryptically.

"When Adam goes back to school in a few weeks, we'll need someone here for Alphie." Albert leaned forward to pet his dog and was rewarded with kisses. "We'd like to have you get started now, though, so we can see how Alphonse responds to you. We need to be sure he's satisfied with his new walker."

"Of course," Maddie said. "That's similar to what I was doing with Howard and Goliath." At the mention of Howard's name, she examined both men's faces for any signs of guilt. She didn't really know what sort of expression to expect from a killer being reminded of his victim, but it didn't matter. Neither man did more than frown, which could be easily explained by thoughts of a man they both hated. It certainly wasn't ironclad evidence of their culpability.

They spent a few moments working out a schedule and going over the contract that they would hopefully sign at the end of her trial week. Maddie was determined to know by then if Adam had killed Howard, so she decided to press a little further.

"One more thing before I go." Adam and Albert both looked at her expectantly, and Maddie cleared her throat and tried to appear meek. "I wanted to apologize." Again the men shared the same expression, this time of curiosity. "The other day at Gwendolyn's party, I behaved poorly. I just want to assure you that I love all dogs, no matter their heritage." She reached over to pet Alphonse for emphasis.

The men seemed bemused by her apology. It was clearly unexpected, and she hoped she could make their surprise work in her favor.

"I was still so upset about Howard. I don't know how much Gwendolyn told you, but I'm the one who found him. I took Goliath for a walk, and when I came back, Howard was dead. I was only out for twenty minutes. Can you imagine if I had come back—" She gasped and paused for dramatic effect and to take inventory of her audience's reaction.

Albert placed a strong hand on her arm and gave it a reassuring squeeze. His brow was furrowed in concern, and she felt in her gut that he couldn't be the killer. Her gut wasn't evidence, but she truly believed that he must be innocent. Adam, however, had blanched during her story, and now he seemed almost terrified. She wondered why.

"Anyway, I let my emotions overtake me, and I spoke without thinking. I just can't believe anyone would want to hurt Howard. He was such a sweet, kind man. Can you imagine hating someone enough to kill him?"

Albert frowned, Adam looked nauseous, and Maddie grew nervous. She interpreted Adam's responses as guilt of some kind, but she couldn't be sure what might be making him feel so overwrought. Was it murder? Or was it his callous gratification at the death of another human being? She wasn't sure she could make him reveal the source of his turmoil, and she knew she could be putting herself in danger by continuing to probe, but she felt she was too close to a breakthrough to stop.

She slapped her head, realizing too late that she might be laying it on a bit thick. "I just remembered—Adam, you didn't like Howard."

Adam had looked guilty before, but now he seemed on the verge of swooning. He was pale and sweating and could do little more than stammer.

"He's not the only one." Albert came to his partner's rescue. His voice was cool and businesslike. "Howard treated us, and several others, poorly. He was a manipulative, self-serving snake, and the only reason you thought of him as sweet and kind is because someone murdered him before he had the chance to screw you over. You should be grateful."

"You think I should appreciate a vicious murder that I almost walked in on?"

"I'm sorry you went through that experience, but neither one of us is sorry that Howard Monk is dead, and if we knew who was responsible, we would be thanking him."

Maddie found it impossible to look away from Albert's intense stare. Though he hadn't admitted to anything, his actions suggested that, if Adam was guilty, Albert knew. Moreover, he'd be more likely to protect Adam than turn him in, a thought that terrified Maddie.

CHAPTER EIGHTEEN

Two blocks away from Adam and Albert's house, Maddie pulled over to collect herself. She wasn't sure how she'd let the conversation get so out of control, but she knew she'd crossed a line. She had come within an inch of accusing Adam of murder, even though her only proof was that he didn't like the victim and had an open schedule on the morning that Howard died. She'd gotten so excited by the pursuit of information and her seeming success that she had clumsily revealed both her interest in finding out who killed Howard and that she suspected Adam. Given her not-very-sly maneuver, they probably surmised that she'd met with them less to woo them as clients than to snoop— disingenuous behavior that had offended Albert.

Though his was a reserved anger—no yelling or lashing out with violence—the look in his eyes had chilled her. She'd never before been on the receiving end of such an intense yet reserved hostility. Equally as chilling as Albert's wrath was Maddie's certainty that it sprang from his protective love for Adam. Maddie understood the intense love and devotion that drove

Albert to defend his partner, but not to this twisted extreme. During her most intense (and unhealthy, she reminded herself) relationship, she had sunk to depressing lows, but even then, she doubted that she would have been willing to harbor a murderer, if that's even what Albert was doing. So while she still wasn't sure about Adam and Albert's involvement in Howard's death, and even though they hadn't threatened her (or fired her for that matter), she couldn't stop trembling for several minutes.

Once she calmed herself enough to drive, she made it another three blocks before her phone rang. Hoping it was the call she'd been obsessing over since going to bed the night before, Maddie pulled over again to answer. She never used her cell phone while driving, but even if she did, she doubted the wisdom of trying to operate a vehicle while also having a coherent and not awkward or embarrassing conversation with a woman who turned her into a timid basket case.

She was disappointed to see Dottie's number on the screen instead of Nadia's. Still, because Dottie refused to talk to machines, Maddie answered, mostly to avoid repeated call attempts and accusations of neglect.

"Just waking up?" Maddie asked.

"Yes, precious. I had an eventful evening. My escort is teeming with potential."

Maddie, accustomed to Dottie's post-date report cards, waited for the explanation she knew was coming.

"He meets all of my criteria—financial, physical and social—and he didn't even mind that I was late. God help him, he thought it was charming."

"If he's captivated by tardiness, he's definitely a keeper."

"Speaking of me being late last night, how was your date? Were you just what the doctor ordered?"

"We had a nice time. She's going to call me later," Maddie answered, ignoring Dottie's joke and hoping to evade conversation about it more successfully than she had with Granny.

"So, did she cure what ails you?" Dottie asked, sounding amused with herself.

"Oh my god, I'm hanging up on you if you keep that up."

"All right, party pooper," Dottie said. "I'll stop."

"Thank you." Then, to keep Dottie off the subject of romance, Maddie launched into the story of her meeting with Adam and Albert.

"I bet Albert's temper brought out a roguish nobility in him. He's such a gallant man."

"I think you're missing the point, Dottie."

"No, I'm choosing to focus on the silver-haired lining rather than the dark cloud. You'd prefer it if I point out that even though you put yourself at risk, you learned almost nothing of value?"

"No, thank you. I don't really need that reminder."

"What if I suggest that now you either have to talk to Ruth Charles again, or you have to give up your investigation? Would that suit you better?"

"I hadn't even considered that. Ugh. Could this day get any worse?"

"I'm sure it could," Dottie said. "You could spontaneously combust. Unflattering clothes could be outlawed. You could be struck on the head, get amnesia and forget about me. "

"Please stop."

"I could go back to harassing you about your new sweetheart."

"Let's not go there either."

Maddie managed to end the call shortly thereafter, and with no further interruptions, she made it home fifteen minutes later. She had greeted the dogs and changed from her business casual, meet-new-clients attire into worn, comfortable jeans and a tank top when the clatter of glass shattering drew her attention to the front of her home. Even before she knew what happened, she knew it was somehow Dottie's fault for tempting the fates with her partial list of things that could go wrong.

Dashing in the direction of the noise, Maddie found a brick on her living room floor, surrounded by shards of what used to be her front window. Heedless of the threat that the shattered glass posed to her bare feet, she ran to the broken window to look for the guilty party, but there was no sign of anything amiss on the street outside—no one speeding away in a car or on foot, none of her neighbors milling about on the sidewalk, angling for the scoop. Maddie couldn't believe that, in broad daylight, someone hurled a brick through her window, and not one person had been out on the street to witness it. Whoever did this was incredibly bold and had gotten away. Then her phone rang.

"Stay out of it," a voice hissed before the line went dead. Though she could be deluding herself, Maddie thought the voice matched the harassing call she'd gotten the other day.

Meanwhile, the dogs had followed her, barking frantically, and now stood with her in a minefield of glass. She lifted Bart and carried him to her bedroom with Goliath on her heels. Neither dog stopped barking, not even as she inspected their feet, which were miraculously uninjured. Assured that the boys were unharmed, at least physically, she considered her next move. She needed to deal with the situation unaided, so she locked them in the room. Their ferocious noise slipped into distressed howling as the door clicked behind her.

On her way back to her living room, she noticed blood on the floor. It had to be hers, but she felt no pain at the moment. She also realized that she needed to call the police, as soon as possible, but hesitated as she reached for her phone. Certainly, this constituted an emergency, but there was the obvious connection to Howard's murder to consider. That meant calling Fitzwilliam, which meant fessing up about her pathetic attempts at crime solving. She supposed, however, that she didn't have to be the one to tell him. She could go through the normal channels followed by other people faced with an emergency, and word would eventually reach Fitzwilliam even if she left him out of the loop. But how long would that take? She wanted Howard's killer and her harasser behind bars now.

"Fitzwilliam." He already sounded irritated, and Maddie suspected that would be his emotional high point in this conversation.

"Detective, this is Matilda Smithwick."

"To what do I owe the pleasure, Miss Smithwick?" He seemed to emphasize his mispronunciation. Maddie decided that he had to be doing it on purpose.

"Someone threw a brick through my window," she began.

"That's terrible." Fitzwilliam sounded a little too sympathetic. His tone bordered on sarcasm. "I hope you weren't hurt."

"I'm fine," she said. "Well, maybe a minor injury, but that's—"

"Listen, Miss Smithwick." Maddie ground her teeth, fighting the urge to strangle him through the phone. "I'm a little busy at the moment solving murders, but there's a special number you can call and get your vandalism issue taken care of right away. It's nine-one-one. I can give that to you again if you need to write it down."

Maddie bit the inside of her cheek to keep from answering with a sarcastic comment of her own. "Thank you, detective, but there's actually more to it than that."

She could almost feel the apprehension and disapproval in his heavy sighs as she told her story, but she left nothing out. From her conversation with Shelly Monk to her meeting with Adam and Albert, she filled the detective in on everything. Once she got it all out, she felt better. Her relief was short-lived.

"Obviously my intellectual skills are inadequate," he grumbled. "So let me see if I understand this. You knew that this matter was under investigation—an investigation by a trained professional with years of experience and the resources of the police department at his disposal, correct?"

"Yes." She felt like a child being chastised and threw in a meek "Sir" to appease him.

"But you decided that, as a dog walker and generally aggravating person with no crime-solving experience outside of reading an Agatha Christie novel, you could do a better job than the police. Is that about right?"

"Yes," she answered and again offered a belated "Sir."

"You also lied about your activities, correct?"

"Yes."

"So you jeopardized my investigation and put yourself in harm's way, and all you have to show for it is a busted window. And now you want me to fix it."

"I don't need you to fix anything, Detective Fitzwilliam." Maddie grew angry at the detective's condescending tone.

Obviously she'd made a mistake. She had naively interfered when she should have minded her own business, and he had reprimanded her appropriately, but it wasn't like she was the murderer. "More than anything right now, I want to start cleaning up the mess in my living room, but I thought this information might be important, detective, maybe even helpful to your investigation. That's why I called you. I was trying to help."

A sharp bark of laughter pierced her ear. "I can't wait until I can retire and get away from all of this help," Fitzwilliam said. After a bit more grousing about Maddie's interference, he relented. "I am tied up right now, but I'll see if I can convince one of my colleagues to swing by your place and check things out. Maybe one of these kids who's going to be doing my job when I'm spending my days fishing in Florida. Ahh," he sighed, and it seemed to Maddie that he either forgot that she was listening, or he was enjoying one last bit of complaining. "No snow, no helpful citizens, none of this garbage."

"How long will it take?"

"I'm not really sure, Miss Smithwick. These things can be hard to judge. Just sit tight."

Maddie suspected she had a wait ahead of her, courtesy of Fitzwilliam's aggravation and need to assert his power. She didn't know if she should clean up the mess in her living room or leave it as evidence, but there were plenty of other things she could take care of in the meantime. The first order of business was to pull the piece of glass, which she now felt with every step, out of her foot. The cut, in the ball of her left foot, was smaller than it felt. However, she realized, upon removing the glass, that the cut was deep, possibly deep enough to consult a medical professional, but she didn't have time for that at the moment. Instead, she cleaned the wound, wincing as the hydrogen peroxide hit it, then covered it with gauze and some cotton balls as a cushion and hoped for the best.

She didn't want to trap the dogs, now whining full force, in the bedroom indefinitely, so she let them into the backyard, where they would stay until it was safe to bring them inside. Bart dashed around for a few minutes, barking at everything. Then, as if assured that he had secured the area, he set to rolling on his back and eating grass. Goliath, on the other hand, skulked out of the house, nervous and whimpering. He immediately lay down near the door and trembled. Maddie stroked his fur gently and spoke to him in soft, reassuring tones, but it did little to abate his nervousness. Damn. Just when he had started to improve, this had to happen.

Though she thought she should be on the lookout for the police, she stayed near Goliath for a few minutes while she called her father—she might as well get the ball rolling on the necessary repairs. Of course, she should have anticipated his severe reaction to the news, but she'd been too rattled to think that far in advance. She finally reassured him that she was fine and that it was more important for him to be with her mother and Granny. She also asked him to keep the news to himself for now, and he reluctantly agreed.

"Looks like you'll be getting those replacement windows sooner than you thought, kiddo," he joked before ending the call.

Almost immediately, her phone rang. Finally, when Maddie had stopped hoping every five seconds for the call and didn't have the time or presence of mind to savor it, Nadia called.

"I'm sorry I didn't call sooner," Nadia said. "It's been crazy here today. My last appointment ended an hour ago, and this is the first chance I've had to sit down."

"A hectic Saturday at a vet's office? I don't believe it," Maddie said. Apparently there was at least one upside to the turmoil surrounding Maddie: it somehow eliminated her awkwardness.

"So," Nadia said, sounding a bit timid. "Can I see you tonight?"

"I would love to see you tonight, but someone decided to throw a brick through my front window, and now I have to wait for the cops to get here."

"Oh my god! Are you all right?"

"I am, but Goliath is terrified. He's trembling and whining in the backyard, and I just can't leave him here while he's so upset. I'm sorry."

"Of course. I understand completely," Nadia said, sounding at least as compassionate as she was disappointed.

Maddie should have expected such sympathy from Nadia, and it made her long for their next encounter even more.

"You know," Nadia said, "it might be a good idea to have a doctor take a look at Goliath, just to make sure he's okay."

"Should I call your office to make an appointment?" Maddie asked, hoping she sounded more flirty than practical.

"I think it should be sooner than that," Nadia said. "The sooner the better, I'm thinking."

"Like this evening, maybe?"

"I could be there in half an hour, if that works."

"That sounds perfect to me."

"Me too," Nadia said.

In another ten minutes a squad car pulled up in front of Maddie's house. She stood at her front door, not sure if she should go out to meet the officer or wait for him to come to her. She couldn't make out any of the officer's features from this distance, though she could tell that he was alone. Maybe this was one of the many officers without partners she saw driving around the city, or maybe Fitzwilliam just didn't place much importance on her broken window. Either way she expected this cop to be just as gruff and unpleasant as Fitzwilliam.

If appearances weren't deceiving, Maddie was not about to get what she expected.

CHAPTER NINETEEN

Maddie watched the cop as she travelled the short distance from her car to the door, enthralled by the view before her. She looked to be about Maddie's size, which made Maddie question the wisdom and safety of allowing her to patrol alone. However, this woman exuded so much confidence that she seemed somehow larger and more powerful than other women of her height and build. She didn't come off as cocky or arrogant, just assured, like she was good at her job and knew it. Maddie suspected that the less upstanding element in the neighborhood knew it too.

The cop had put her glossy black hair in a small, tight bun that popped through the hole in her police baseball cap, and even with only that much to go on, Maddie thought it would be soft and wonderful to touch. Though her eyes were hidden by sunglasses, her face, with its full, pouty lips and perfect nose suggested to Maddie that this woman could just as easily have been a model as a cop.

"Please," Maddie prayed to no one in particular, "please let her be at least as disagreeable as Fitzwilliam. Otherwise I'm in big trouble."

She sighed heavily and opened the door. Up close and without her sunglasses, the cop was even better looking, and Maddie could tell that she was of at least partial Asian descent. Maddie couldn't be more specific, and it seemed wrong to ask. First, it would be rude—no matter how she phrased the question, it would come off sounding like, "Hey, you're obviously different. Care to explain?" It was also none of her business and completely beside the point.

"So, I hear you had a little accident." Thankfully, the cop seemed cool and somewhat distant, but her low, sweet voice drew Maddie in. The woman grew more attractive by the second, and it took Maddie half a beat to regain her senses and answer.

"I'm not sure this falls under the heading of 'accident.'"

The hot cop's laughter, an easy, delightful sound, eradicated most of her aloofness and threatened to send Maddie over the edge. It was ridiculous—she had gone years without the slightest interest in romance, and now she was drooling over every woman who crossed her path. It didn't help that so many of the women who ended up on her path lately were insanely beautiful—how was she supposed to restrain herself? Then again, there were worse problems to have. Maddie decided to blame her visceral response to this woman on last night's heated encounter with Nadia, and Maddie's subsequent thoughts of her. There was nothing more to it.

"Walk me through what happened."

"I was in the bedroom with my dogs."

Maddie blushed as she remembered that she'd taken off her bra when she changed, and even though her breasts were small, the snug, white tank top she wore did nothing to conceal her bralessness.

Crossing her arms over her chest, she continued. "I heard glass breaking and ran out here where I found this." Still trying to cover her chest, she gestured awkwardly at the mess on her floor.

"When was that?"

Maddie looked at her watch. "About an hour ago."

"Did you see anyone?"

"No. By the time I got to the window, whoever did this was gone. But someone called right away, threatened me and hung up."

"Do you have the number on your phone?" The officer seemed hopeful.

Maddie shook her head. "It said 'unknown.'"

The cop nodded solemnly then asked, "What about your neighbors? Did any of them see anything?"

"I don't think so. There was no one outside when I looked." And if there was one thing she could count on her neighbors for, it was swarming the scene of any excitement, good or bad.

"I have to be honest with you." The cop sighed and rested her hands on her hips, which looked good even in typically unflattering police uniform pants. "Our chances of finding whoever did this aren't very good."

"Can't you just fingerprint the brick?"

"You've seen too many episodes of *CSI*." The cop smiled indulgently at Maddie, who tried to ignore the tremor in her stomach. "Even if we could get a decent print, there's no guarantee it would match anything in the system."

"Oh," Maddie said, feeling disappointed. She'd hoped that the killer had made a crucial mistake, but of course it couldn't be that simple.

"And even if we got lucky with getting a print and finding a match, it would really only prove that the person touched the brick, which isn't a crime."

"Oh," Maddie repeated, crestfallen.

"But I can have an evidence technician come out if you want. It'll probably be a bit of a wait, though, and you'll have a bigger mess to deal with by the time it's all over."

"And it won't amount to anything?"

"Probably not, but there's always a chance." The cop seemed eager to make Maddie feel better.

"Forget it, then. I'm sorry to have dragged you out here for nothing."

"It's no trouble. This is my beat, so I'm always in the area. I'll keep an eye out for you."

"Thanks," Maddie answered, already thinking about the cleanup.

"I wish I could have done more for you, Miss Smithwick."

"It's Smi—" Out of habit, Maddie started to correct the mispronunciation before realizing it was unnecessary. "I'm sorry. I've never had anybody get my name right on the first try."

The cop grinned. "I grew up hating my name because so many people mangled it. I try not to inflict that on others."

Maddie glanced at the officer's name tag and laughed softly. "I'm sure a lot of people had a difficult time pronouncing Murphy correctly. It must have been a real trial for you."

"The first name is the troublemaker," Officer Murphy said and winked.

Maddie felt a blush creep up her face. She wanted to ask the cop's first name but decided against it. The less she knew about Officer Murphy the better. Nadia would be showing up soon, and Maddie didn't think she could handle more than one flourishing crush on a stunning woman at a time.

Apparently enjoying her effect on Maddie, Officer Murphy now seemed to want to linger. "You're a dog walker, right? Do you ever take care of cats?"

"Dogs, cats, fish, a ferret once. We do it all." Maddie paused to procure a business card, and a thought occurred to her. "How did you know I'm a dog walker?"

"Fitz told me."

"Detective Fitzwilliam?" Murphy nodded. "He's a real charmer."

"Fitz isn't bad once you get to know him."

"I'm sure," Maddie drawled.

"I've learned a lot from him. He's been a great mentor."

"Just don't take any behavioral cues from him."

Murphy laughed. "Fitz definitely has his moods, but he's a good cop. He follows the evidence, doesn't take the easy path or jump to conclusions. He works hard to build a case, and he never makes an arrest unless the evidence supports it. Even then..."

"Even then what?"

"He usually has pretty good instincts about things, so even if the evidence points one way, he might go in a different direction if it doesn't feel right."

"What do you mean?" Maddie couldn't help her curiosity, and she didn't really mind encouraging Officer Murphy's lengthy departure.

Murphy hesitated. She seemed to be deciding how much she could say. "Hypothetically speaking, a lot of evidence might point to a particular suspect. Say her prints are on the murder weapon, and she's the only person that any witnesses saw entering or leaving the crime scene. Maybe she even found the body but didn't call the cops right away." Officer Murphy looked at Maddie intently.

"That sounds like pretty damning evidence." Maddie gulped involuntarily. Somehow Dottie was right—Maddie was suspected of murder.

"It is, but Fitz wouldn't necessarily be convinced, that is, if he ever had a case like that, which I'm not suggesting. But if he did, he would probably say he doesn't feel it in his gut."

A wave of relief washed over Maddie. She would have to be nice to Detective Fitzwilliam if she ever encountered him again.

"When there's really no motive, like in that case, Fitz keeps exploring his options."

Finding her voice, Maddie said, "You're right. He does sound like a good cop."

"I'll tell him you said so." She grinned and winked at Maddie again.

They stood in silence for a moment before Officer Murphy reiterated her offer to keep an eye on Maddie. "I'll give you a call some time—" she held up the card Maddie had given her "—if I ever need a cat sitter."

Alone again, Maddie took a moment to check on the dogs. Bart had joined Goliath on the deck just outside the door, where they lay curled up together with Goliath's head resting on Bart's flank. Maddie stooped to reassure them that they'd be back inside soon, and as she petted them she noticed that Goliath's trembling had subsided. He didn't seem eager about life at the moment, but at least he no longer looked terrified.

As she swept up the glass, her thoughts bounced around frantically, touching upon most of the topics currently weighing on her mind. Deciding that she had too quickly dismissed her father's offer to help, she looked at the shattered glass and the storm clouds outside her broken window. Then her mind turned to excited thoughts of Nadia's imminent arrival before succumbing to confused speculation about her conversation with Officer Murphy.

She had told Maddie (or, more accurately, broadly hinted to her) that Fitzwilliam didn't seriously consider her guilty of Howard's murder. Maddie had never believed she was a suspect, but now that she knew she had been, it was a relief to know that she was mostly in the clear. While she appreciated that relief, she wondered about the risk Murphy took by speaking to her, even hypothetically, about the investigation. Maddie imagined she could get in a lot of trouble for that, not that Maddie would tell, but Officer Murphy had no way of knowing that. Murphy could always deny discussing specifics of the case—and it would be true—but it seemed like a giant gamble to take. Maddie hadn't a clue what had motivated it.

The closer it got to Nadia's arrival, the more oddly guilty Maddie felt about her encounter with Officer Murphy, though Maddie hadn't done anything wrong, not really. While she hadn't discouraged Officer Murphy's flirtation, she also hadn't flirted back. And even if she had, why should she feel bad about it? She'd had one date with Nadia and was free to flirt with anyone she chose. Still, it felt deceitful to play the coquette with one woman while waiting for the next to appear.

And she was excited about seeing Nadia again. She wished she could offer a better second date than window repair and dog care followed by a meal from one of the finer dining establishments in the area that delivered. She would have cooked for Nadia, but a brick through her window had cancelled her trip to the grocery store, and she doubted that Nadia would enjoy a wilted lettuce salad with a side of matured condiments.

Just then, the cause of Maddie's excitement appeared at her door. Maddie suspected that she'd stopped home to clean up a bit—her hair was still damp, and instead of her adorable scrubs, Nadia wore jeans and a white button-down shirt with rolled up sleeves. They embraced on Maddie's porch, Nadia seemingly as happy to see Maddie as Maddie was to see her. Their kiss was soft but full of promise, and Maddie dragged her inside. It occurred to Maddie that, for the second time in two days, she had invited Nadia into her home, but today the underlying invitation brought on more eagerness than nervousness—a welcome change.

"What do you need?" Nadia asked, surveying first Maddie and then the room. "How can I help?"

"The dogs are outside. I don't want to bring them in until I cover the window, which I can't do alone. I hate to ask—"

"You didn't ask," Nadia said. "I offered."

Maddie kissed her again. She'd only meant to express her gratitude, but it seemed like more than that. "Follow me," she said and grabbed Nadia's hand.

"Anywhere," Nadia answered, a little breathless, as Maddie led the way to the basement.

They worked well together. Nadia held the plywood that Maddie had kept—just in case—after she and her father had finished most of the remodeling, while Maddie screwed it in place. As Maddie drilled in the last screw, she glanced at Nadia, who still held the board, though she no longer needed to. She had obviously been watching Maddie, and her expression could only be described as carnal.

"What?" Maddie asked.

"You're making me want to break stuff so I can watch you do more repairs."

"Really?" Maddie asked, pleased with herself.

She nodded, still entranced. "The lesbian handywoman thing is a definite turn on."

Maddie fought a blush, and picking up the playful vibe, she said, "You should see me in my tool belt." Then taking a cue from both Nadia and Officer Murphy, she winked.

The smoldering look Nadia gave her did wonders for Maddie's confidence and her rapidly building desire. "Let's go get the dogs," she said before she lost herself completely.

As Nadia inspected Bart and Goliath, Maddie ordered their dinner from the hole in the wall restaurant two blocks from Maddie's house. They made the best pizza on the North Side, and Nadia, who said she never ordered pizza for herself, promised a doubtful Maddie that she was looking forward to it, before turning her attention to the boys.

Maddie smiled to see Bart frolicking at Nadia's feet, barely slowing down to let her pet him, let alone get a good look at him. He had obviously already recovered from this afternoon's harrowing ordeal. Goliath, too, seemed to enjoy Nadia's ministrations. He leaned into her hip and grunted as she petted him, and though he didn't join in Bart's joyous dancing, his tail did flutter slightly as Nadia cooed over him.

After several minutes of aggressive doting, Nadia declared both dogs healthy and called the incident a minor setback for Goliath. She assured Maddie that he would eventually return to his usual playfulness. "You're doing great work with him. Keep it up, and he'll be fine."

"Thank you." Maddie moved in for a lingering kiss, enjoying the effect she clearly had on Nadia, whose hands began roaming. She doubted she could find the will to say no if Nadia asked for more than kisses. She was on the verge of asking herself when their dinner arrived.

Both women managed to feign interest in their meal long enough to take a bite.

"It's really hot," Nadia said, her eyes locked on Maddie's.

"We should probably give it some time to cool." Maddie didn't even realize she was moving toward Nadia until their lips met. Then Nadia's strong hands were in her hair, drawing her closer, and pizza was the last thing on Maddie's mind.

Somehow they made it from the dining room to the bedroom without breaking their kiss. Nadia's hands travelled across Maddie's breasts and down to her waist. Hooking her index fingers through the belt loops of Maddie's jeans, she roughly pulled Maddie even closer.

"Please tell me you're ready now."

"God yes," Maddie answered and brought her mouth back to Nadia's, their tongues volleying before Maddie bit Nadia's lip playfully. "Are you?"

In answer Nadia removed Maddie's shirt and threw it to the floor. Her lips moved to Maddie's breasts, tasting first one, then the other as she guided her to the bed. Certain she would explode from this minor contact, Maddie let out a small groan as she lay back with Nadia straddling her. Her hands reached up to unbutton Nadia's shirt and feel the soft warmth of her skin. Through Nadia's bra, she cupped her breasts, enjoying the fullness of them, eager to explore further. How had she gone so long without this?

Nadia's hands seemed to be everywhere, massaging, exploring and teasing as her mouth latched onto Maddie's breast, rolling her hardened nipple in her mouth, further igniting the desire within Maddie. The incredible sensations coursing through her body were at war with her mind. Usually her first time with someone was clouded with worries—that her breasts were too small, that she had too many freckles, that she was, in hundreds of other ways, inadequate. Her brain catalogued every flaw, real or imagined, from the moment that her clothing started to come off.

This time was no different, and as she struggled to quiet the anxiety, Nadia's mouth left Maddie's breast. Her tongue traced the planes of Maddie's abdomen, and her hands tugged at the button of Maddie's jeans, urging her to give more of herself. She removed the remainder of Maddie's clothes, paused to take an appraising look, and with two words, ended any remaining trace of Maddie's self-criticism.

"You're beautiful."

"Kiss me," Maddie said, and as their lips met, Maddie wrapped her naked legs around Nadia's thighs, drawing her close. Soon, they fell into a rhythm, the intensity of Maddie's arousal building even as Nadia withheld her touch. Maddie was sure the anticipation alone would be her undoing. Bliss verged on anguish, and when Nadia finally touched Maddie, it took only a few deft strokes before a deep, satisfied moan escaped her, and she crested the wave.

CHAPTER TWENTY

At Goliath's persistent urging, a bleary-eyed Maddie rose before seven to tend to the dogs. She was a little surprised that he'd let her sleep in, so to speak. She had fed him and his foster brother before letting them out in the yard around eleven the night before, but Maddie (feeling guilty all the while) had been too selfish to get fully dressed and take the boys for their usual nighttime walk around the neighborhood. She'd made sure their basic needs were met, but she'd given them little more than half an hour of her undivided attention since Nadia had showed up the night before. She knew she would have to make it up to them and soon.

Gazing sleepily out the window while Bart and Goliath ate, Maddie admired the clear blue sky that held the promise of a beautiful day. Maddie thought she would take the boys somewhere fun to appreciate it, maybe one of the forest preserves for a walk through nature. Bart loved exploring the trails, and she thought that Goliath might enjoy the outing as well. She wasn't sure how well he'd behave in her Jeep now that he was moving away from his depressed moping, but perhaps she could convince Nadia to join them. She could help monitor the dogs in the car, and it would be nice to spend the day together.

Maddie rolled her eyes at herself, appalled by her premature clinginess. After only two dates, it was a little early to become so wrapped up in Nadia. Not that Nadia made it difficult to get attached. Even before the sex, Maddie had been captivated by Nadia. After last night, she was in danger of becoming a lovesick nitwit. It was a possibility she found more agreeable than terrifying.

Neither pup paid much attention to his breakfast, so Maddie finally relented and ushered them into the backyard, where puddles and broken branches told her that it had rained again. She had been too preoccupied to notice the storm as it happened, but she appreciated its effects. The temperature had fallen again. It was almost cool compared to the previous week, so she allowed the boys to linger in the yard and enjoy themselves.

At her father's insistence, Maddie's yard had a six-foot-high privacy fence with a secure lock. The dogs couldn't escape without hours of focused effort, and no one could get in without a ladder, the code to unlock the gate or some noisy equipment to dismantle the fence. She knew the boys, who were chewing on sticks and chasing one another around the yard, the tumult of yesterday forgotten, would be safe by themselves for a while, so she left them to their amusement.

But when she went back inside, eager to brush her teeth and make herself presentable before Nadia woke up, she realized what the dogs had been up to the night before when she was too engrossed in other activities to notice. She couldn't believe she'd missed it her first time through the house, but she hadn't exactly been alert: the dinner that she and Nadia had rejected in favor of other pursuits had not been so readily overlooked by the dogs. The now torn and empty pizza box had been dragged off the table (the height of which would be no challenge for a dog Goliath's size), and aside from a few stray pieces of crust on a chair and some crumbs scattered about the floor, the food was gone. No wonder they had ignored breakfast. She groaned in irritation, but she couldn't be mad at the dogs—they had only seized the opportunity that Maddie shouldn't have given them. Frustrated with herself, she swept up the evidence of the dogs' mischief and headed back outside with the garbage.

When she saw what Bart and Goliath had been up to while she was cleaning up their earlier mess, she bemoaned the distraction that had once more allowed the dogs to be dogs. During their brief span of unsupervised yard time, they'd found the muddiest corner and turned it into their romping headquarters. They'd flung mud and clumps of grass halfway up the fence, and they were so filthy that she could see more mud than fur coating their legs and backs. When they bounded up to her, tails wagging and tongues lolling out the sides of their mouths, she knew it would be a bath day. She hoped that Howard's likely grooming regimen for Goliath meant that he tolerated baths better than Bart did. For all his easygoing, nearly perfect dog charms, Bart was a nightmare when it came to baths, and if Goliath behaved as poorly as Bart at bath time, Maddie was going to need a bigger bathtub, more towels, a few extra hands and half her day. So much for a fun outing with Nadia and the boys.

Not yet ready to confront the task of bathing the dogs, Maddie opted to let them stay outside and get dirtier. The damage was already done, and they were obviously enjoying themselves. Plus, if Nadia was still asleep, she wouldn't be once Bart waged his anti-bath campaign. Maddie could think of several better ways to wake up than the forlorn howling of a filthy dog.

But Maddie needn't have worried. By the time she made it back to the bedroom, Nadia was up and almost fully clothed. Given that she was buttoning her shirt like she was trying to set a new speed record for dressing, Maddie automatically wondered if she'd done something wrong. She couldn't immediately think of anything, but that didn't stop her brain from trying. Maddie wanted to believe she was being paranoid—both about Nadia trying to flee and about being the reason for her hasty departure—but she had no other explanation for her date's focused dressing. She didn't think she could ask, either.

"Where were you?" Nadia barely paused in her activities when Maddie approached her.

"The dogs," was the only explanation Maddie offered.

"Of course." She nodded curtly as she sat to put on her socks. Nadia was definitely acting a little aloof which didn't ease Maddie's paranoia in the least. "Are they all right?"

"More or less. They're a lot happier now than they will be in an hour."

Nadia raised her eyebrows in a question.

"Unplanned bath day, thanks to their morning mud wrestling."

"Poor kids." Nadia's tone was compassionate, and she shook her head in sympathy.

Maddie, pleased to see Nadia's warmer side, was about to ask about her plans for the day, but she didn't get the chance.

"I should get going."

"So early?" Maddie sank onto the bed. She knew it was too soon to expect Nadia to spend every waking moment with her, but she had hoped they could at least have breakfast together. Apparently that was out of the question.

"I've got a lot to do and only one day to do it in. If I don't start now, I won't finish in time."

"For what?" What could be so pressing that Nadia couldn't stick around long enough for a cup of coffee?

"To see you again tonight." She kissed Maddie's cheek before putting her shoes on.

Maddie wasn't sure how to interpret Nadia's mercurial temperament this morning, but she was satisfied with the more positive turn in her affections. She felt better knowing that, at least for now, she wasn't the only sentimental one in the relationship. Though Maddie longed to figure out the root of Nadia's shifting mood, she had no time to dwell on the matter. She didn't even get the chance to retrieve the dogs from the yard because her dad showed up not five minutes later.

Maddie's immediate reaction was intense relief that he hadn't popped in earlier. Though she was a grown woman, had started her own business, owned her own home and hadn't lived under her parents' roof in several years, she still would have felt like a little girl who'd been caught with her hand in the cookie jar if her dad had crossed paths with her date so early in the morning when it was obvious what they'd been up to. She preferred him to be clueless about her love life (or at least to believe that he was).

Tall and brawny with a graying beard and weathered face, Colm Smithwick was the quintessential picture of a laborer—he could put on a hard hat and blend in at any construction site anywhere. He was also one of those people whose voice didn't match his appearance. He should have had a deep, rumbling voice, something coarse and rough around the edges. Instead he was soft-spoken with a smooth tenor that soothed Maddie.

"You did this yourself?" he asked, admiring her handiwork from the day before as he entered her living room. He tapped the wood, checking its soundness. "Nice job."

Maddie knew her father loved his work—using his hands, wielding tools, finding creative solutions to problems and striving for perfection in every project he undertook were all profoundly satisfying to Mr. Smithwick. Even so, this was strange. "You came over this early on a Sunday to discuss my window?"

"I came to measure it." He pulled out a tape measure and got to work, jotting down the dimensions of the broken window, as well as its neighbors. "We don't want to wait on these replacements. A boarded-up window is an invitation—"

"For mayhem, I know, but I could have done this, Dad. You gave me a tape measure and a level for my sixth birthday, remember?"

"I remember, kiddo, but you had me worried, and this was the best excuse I could think of to come check on you. I wanted to be sure you're okay." His grin stretched across his face, and his eyes twinkled. "I should have known you'd be fine. You're too much like your grandmother not to be." Maddie hugged her dad, appreciating the compliment. "Speaking of which, I can't stay long. She'll spit nails if we're not at the hospital to pick her up on time."

"Granny's being released?"

"Yeah. She finally wore the doctors down, so they're letting her go home. I'm surprised it took so long—she can be a bear when she isn't getting her way."

Filled with relief and excited to be finished with trips to the hospital, Maddie knew she'd be walking over to Granny's house later. She didn't know if she'd get Granny to herself, but the joy of seeing her in her own home was more than enough to satisfy Maddie.

Back to business, her dad tapped on the plywood again. "It'll go faster if you help me out."

Smiling at his single-minded focus, she grabbed the tape measure from his hand and got to work.

They finished quickly, and after her father left, she took a moment to regroup before facing the inevitable. The dogs would just make a bigger mess the longer she waited, and she didn't want to spend her entire Sunday cleaning up after them. She called Goliath to her first because it seemed somehow wiser to start with the unknown. If Goliath was as uncontrollable in the bath as he was on a walk, then she wanted to get it over with. And, by comparison, Bart's bath would be a treat. If by some miracle Goliath actually behaved, well, at least Bart's bath wouldn't be any worse than usual.

Goliath came with her willingly, and Maddie suspected that meant that he just didn't know what he was in for, but if he was surprised by what came next, he didn't show it. He actually jumped into the tub when Maddie told him it was bath time, and he remained accommodating and relaxed throughout the process.

"So you like baths and the vet." Goliath licked her face as if in agreement and then turned himself around to give Maddie easier access to his other side. "You're kind of an odd dog. I don't mean that in a bad way," she amended when Goliath tilted his head to eye her curiously. "Who could blame you for liking your vet? She's very likable. Frustrating and confusing, and I'm not sure she likes *me*, but—" Goliath continued to regard her quizzically, and Maddie realized how ridiculous she was being. Even if Goliath could have a conversation with her, it wasn't like he was her therapist. She needed to quit obsessing over whether Nadia liked her, or why she would.

Consciously moving away from thoughts of her love life as she shampooed the unbelievably obliging dog in her bathtub, she instead began pondering her investigative frustrations. Replaying her conversation with Detective Fitzwilliam, she knew that she should give up her search for answers. She was getting nowhere and putting herself in danger in the process, and as Fitzwilliam pointed out, she had no idea what she was doing. What were her chances of finding Howard's killer if the police hadn't succeeded yet? Was it really worth all the trouble?

She asked Goliath that same question, then answered it herself as he lifted his paw for her to wash it. "If I give up now, I might never know who hurt your dad, but I'll also most likely get through the next week without any property damage or harassing phone calls. That would be nice."

She could let her life get back to normal and focus on other matters—her budding relationship with Nadia, getting Goliath past his depression and into a new home and making sure Granny's health continued to improve. Granny and Dottie would probably give Maddie a hard time about quitting. Then again, if they knew about the brick through her window, they might call her crazy for wanting to continue.

But, she realized as she massaged conditioner into Goliath's fur, she *did* want to continue. She knew she would never stop wondering who was behind Howard's death and her week from hell. She couldn't stand the thought of someone getting away with killing Howard and making her life miserable.

"I have to know who did it, Goliath," she told him as she rinsed him.

Even though it was in her best interests to make peace with Howard's death and move on, she refused to let it go. If she was discreet enough, maybe then the killer would think she had been frightened off. She would be safe and could find the answers she needed.

The decision to forge ahead made, Maddie allowed her thoughts to drift to her conversation with the alluring Officer

Murphy. She still couldn't believe that Murphy had revealed so much to her, but she was grateful to know that Fitzwilliam and a SWAT team wouldn't be storming her home to arrest her for murder any time soon. Of course, before yesterday, it hadn't occurred to her that her actions (completely innocent in her mind) would make her suspicious in the eyes of the police, though somehow Dottie had known. She could explain all of it so easily: her presence at Howard's, her instinct to call Dottie rather than the police—

Maddie stopped. A realization dawned on her, and she almost slapped her forehead.

"I'm such an idiot," she said to the patient creature dripping in her tub.

This whole time she had thought that Howard was beaten to death with his walking stick. It had been beside him when she found him, so she had assumed the killer had used it, but she was wrong.

She grabbed a towel and patted Goliath inattentively.

"I have to call Dottie," she told him and left the bathroom, a still damp Goliath padding after her.

CHAPTER TWENTY-ONE

"Is your watch broken? Have all of the clocks in your home stopped?" The resounding vexation in Dottie's voice made Maddie cringe. "Maybe you're in some sort of dimensional wormhole where time has ceased. Or perhaps you have what you consider a very good reason for calling before ten on a Sunday morning."

Maddie had expected Dottie's petulance (though she'd hoped for a watered-down version of what she was getting), and she knew better than to try to answer any of her friend's rhetorical questions. They were for dramatic effect only, so she let Dottie continue unimpeded.

"What might have inspired you to call me at this hour? Have you stumbled yet again upon another victim of a grisly murder? Have you impaled yourself? Are you on fire or otherwise in need of my immediate assistance?"

Maddie refrained from pointing out how useless Dottie was in a medical emergency, especially since she sounded oddly hopeful as she rattled off potential calamities that might have befallen Maddie. Instead she tried to get to the point. "I need to talk about dog shows."

"Now? I have tried for years to cultivate your appreciation for loftier pursuits, and at dawn on a Sunday you spontaneously take an interest? Maybe next weekend we could chat about the opera or Burberry's fall line while we're not getting our beauty rest."

Maddie paced in her kitchen as she half-listened to Dottie's wounded rant. Anxious to move past her friend's self-indulgent diatribe, Maddie jumped in with an apology as soon as Dottie's need for oxygen offered her the chance to speak.

"I'm sorry about my timing, Dottie, but this information could help me figure out who killed Howard." She knew Dottie would be hooked by the prospect of her own importance, so she stroked Dottie's ego further. "I wanted to contact you before you got caught up in all the other demands on your time."

Silence. Maddie could picture Dottie's face morphing from vexation and bewilderment to vainglorious intrigue as she processed this information.

"Very well." Dottie sighed heavily, and in her head Maddie celebrated her minor victory. "Give me an hour to get rid of my company and prepare myself for the day."

"Thank you, Dottie," Maddie said, calculating that she had at least ninety minutes before Dottie made her appearance. That should give her plenty of time to bathe Bart, undo the wreckage that that misadventure would cause to her bathroom and get herself cleaned up. If she hurried, she might even have a chance to run to the store before Dottie arrived.

Maybe Goliath had warned Bart telepathically, or maybe he noticed Goliath's damp fur, smelled the shampoo and drew his own conclusions. Whatever the cause, Bart put up more of a struggle over this bath than ever before. He was like an animated dog, howling wildly, planting his feet and refusing to move so that Maddie either had to drag him by his collar or carry him. Hating the idea of pulling a dog by his neck and not loving the idea of leaving muddy track marks from her back door to her bathroom, she opted to carry him. When they reached the bathroom, he splayed his legs, grabbing the doorframe and preventing their entry for several minutes before Maddie could maneuver him through the door. It was worse than trying to get a sleeper sofa up three narrow, winding flights of stairs.

Still unwilling to give up the fight even after they were locked in the bathroom, Bart barked at the door, whined at Maddie and scratched at the marble tiles of the floor, apparently trying to dig his way to freedom, while Maddie got the tub ready for him.

"Sorry buddy," she spoke in soothing tones, "but you're filthy. You know the rules—you play, you pay."

He barked once more and stared at her from under his shaggy eyebrows. If dog expressions could speak, Bart's would be saying, "How could you? I trusted you!"

But Maddie, feeling no guilt over her betrayal, set him in the tub and got to work rinsing away the layers of grime as he whined.

"You know," she told him, "some people consider this a treat."

He whimpered again, obviously not experiencing the joy of a warm bath.

"I guess it loses something without a good book and a drink."

By the time they finished, Bart had pulled the stopper from the drain once and jumped out of the tub twice, dousing Maddie and the room in gray, soapy water. Maddie was exhausted, but she wasn't done yet. She still had to return her bathroom to something fit for human use, groom herself to circumvent any ridicule from her image-conscious friend and find some sort of Sunday brunch offering to appease Dottie. Given Dottie's nutritive proclivities, Maddie could probably skip the omelet and coffee cake, instead supply a pitcher of Bloody Marys with a straw and earn Dottie's heartfelt gratitude (if such an action wasn't so uncouth).

A little over an hour later, Dottie walked into the kitchen just as Maddie was pouring her cocktail—a sparkling tarragon gin lemonade that Maddie thought would be a light, refreshing alternative to typical brunch offerings. After returning from the grocery store, Maddie had left her front door unlocked so that

Dottie could let herself in, a liberty she would take anyway, so why not just roll with the inevitable, Maddie thought.

Dottie took a sip and smiled appreciatively. "If the dog walking falls through, you can always make it as a bartender," she said.

"Thanks for the vote of confidence." Sipping her own drink, Maddie had to agree it was delicious.

"What happened out front? Unspeakable accident or impulsive remodeling project?"

"Neither," Maddie answered, remembering that the last time she'd spoken to Dottie her home had been intact. A lot had happened since then. "Howard's killer tried to discourage me by launching a brick through my window."

"And it didn't work?" Dottie's eyes grew large as Maddie shook her head. "Sunshine, this is getting dangerous."

"Which is why I need to find the killer, and soon. Will you help me?"

"Of course," Dottie said, in one of her rare moments of sincerity. She settled herself at Maddie's dining room table and asked, "What do you need?"

"I need to know everything you know about Goliath's dog show trophy." Maddie grabbed the pitcher of drinks and joined her friend at the table. She didn't know how lubricated Dottie would have to be for this conversation, but she was ready for anything.

"The trophy? What does the trophy have to do with this?"

"It was the murder weapon."

"What?" Dottie shrieked and clutched her chest dramatically. "Someone bludgeoned Howard to death with that monstrosity? How do you know?"

Maddie recounted her conversation with Officer Murphy, smiling a little at the memory of Murphy's easy, flirtatious manner. "I had thought that the killer used Howard's walking stick—it would've been like swinging a baseball bat, and Howard couldn't have put up much of a fight to keep it from the killer. It would make a great weapon."

"Are you *sure* you didn't do it?"

Maddie glared at Dottie for a minute before continuing. "Officer Murphy hinted that my fingerprints were on the murder weapon, but I never touched that cane. I did touch the trophy."

"I see," Dottie drew the words out, obviously contemplating something. "Let me ask you this—just how attractive is this Officer Murphy?"

"What?" Maddie was stunned by the question. She feigned innocence. "Why would you ask that?"

"You're flushed and smiling while discussing Howard's grisly death. Either you've lost all sense of propriety, or you're thinking of something much more delectable."

Maddie felt her face get hot, and she knew her deep blush must make her look sunburned. There was no denying her crush, but she didn't have to dwell on it either. She pursed her lips and hoped that Dottie would take the hint and move on. No such luck.

"Does Dr. Feelgood know you've got the hots for Chicago's finest's finest?"

Maddie glared at Dottie again. "The subject didn't come up."

"Too busy making out?"

"No," Maddie offered a feeble denial and refused to make eye contact.

"I see things with the vet are going well," Dottie said, sounding far too pleased with herself.

Giving in—it would be easier than struggling to keep Dottie on track—Maddie said, "I hope so."

"What makes you hopeful rather than certain?"

"She was acting a little distant this morning when—"

"When she left!"

Maddie dropped her head on the table. She hadn't meant to divulge that bit of information.

"Congratulations, tiger. I'm so proud of you!"

"Why do I ever tell you anything?"

"Because I am your dearest friend and you love me more than life itself."

"That must be it," Maddie said drily. "Can we get back to the point now?"

"Certainly." Dottie smiled knowingly and topped off her beverage before asking, "Which point is that?"

"The trophy," Maddie groaned, exasperated.

"Ah, yes, the trophy." Dottie took a fortifying swallow of her drink before sharing what she knew.

"I don't know much about its origins. Howard had the trophy when he joined our little group a year or so ago."

Maddie nodded, mulling over that piece of information as Dottie continued.

"I don't remember the specifics, but it was from a show in Colorado."

"Wait. That doesn't add up. If Howard left Colorado when Goliath was a puppy, which is what Shelly told us, how did he win a trophy there? Can puppies compete?"

"As long as Goliath was six months old on the day of the show, Howard could have entered him. Of course, given Howard's inexperience, it's doubtful that he and Goliath would have mastered conformation handling at such a young age." By the gleam in Dottie's eyes, Maddie gathered that she was excited to be imparting her dog show wisdom. "He could have hired a professional handler, but then I think Goliath would have more to show for it."

Apparently Maddie wasn't the only one who'd noticed Goliath's willful independence.

"Assuming Goliath wasn't a puppy when he won, why would Howard go all the way back to Colorado? Why wouldn't he just compete here? Did he ever tell you why?"

"No." Dottie pursed her lips in thought. "He never wanted to talk about the details. He told all of us all the time that Goliath was a champion, but he always avoided getting into the specifics. Come to think of it, I don't believe he entered Goliath in a single show the entire time I knew him."

"This makes no sense. Why would he keep a young champion out of competition?"

Dottie lifted her shoulders elegantly, her version of a shrug and said, "I wish I knew, sweet cheeks, but it is simply unfathomable to me."

While Maddie sat silently, thoughts swirling around her head, Dottie helped herself to another refill. Maddie hoped she had taken a cab because if she kept going at this pace, she'd be sleeping it off in Maddie's spare room.

"What are you thinking, chief?"

"The trophy—from almost every standpoint it makes no sense as a weapon. It's heavy and cumbersome, and it would be awkward to swing at someone, even someone confined to a wheelchair. Then there's the time aspect. The killer had to hurry to be gone before I got back with Goliath, but the trophy wasn't in a convenient space. Wouldn't you just grab the nearest blunt object and swing rather than seeking out an unwieldy ornament?"

"So you think the trophy was significant to the killer," Dottie finished Maddie's thought.

"I do," Maddie said. "I need to find out everything I can about that dog show. I know it's the key to Howard's death."

"How do you plan to do that, kitten? Are you just going to Google 'Colorado dog shows' and hope for the best?"

"It's a start," Maddie spoke confidently as she opened her laptop, but when Google came back with over twelve million results, her confidence disappeared. "How am I going to narrow this down?"

"You could try using Goliath's show name."

Maddie looked at her friend expectantly.

"I don't know it. I told you Howard didn't share the details of Goliath's victory. Don't you have it in your records?"

"Why would *I* have it?" Maddie whined. "My job was to take him to the bathroom, not escort him to Kennel Club victory."

"Didn't Howard include it with his paperwork when he hired you?"

"No, but I know someone who might have it." Maddie said, smiling as a hopeful thought occurred to her. "I have to call Nadia."

"This is hardly the time to tend to your social calendar."

Maddie glared at her friend once more as she reached for her phone.

CHAPTER TWENTY-TWO

Maddie told Dottie to think about what she wanted to eat and then excused herself from the room, leaving her friend to the liquid portion of her meal. While Maddie didn't plan to slip into sappy romantic chatter during this conversation (even though her plans seemed to fall by the wayside more and more where Nadia was concerned), she still needed privacy. Unless she wanted Dottie offering background commentary (which she didn't). Considering that Maddie had plied her with alcohol, Dottie's input was a certainty, not just a hazard.

Maddie closed her bedroom door behind her and sat on the bed. Goliath, who had followed her, now curled up on the floor, his chin resting on her feet. She reached down to pet his head, and he responded with a trilling, coo-like noise she had never before heard from a dog. Then he rolled over to offer up his belly. He seemed to be regaining his confidence and happiness, which pleased Maddie. He was a sweet dog and would be a great addition to someone else's home. She realized she was going to miss him when he was gone.

Unlike Goliath, Bart—still holding a grudge over Maddie's earlier violation—had kept his distance, choosing instead to keep Dottie company. (He had actually turned his back to Maddie as she left the room, and she knew she was supposed to be wounded by this.) They were probably bonding over their shared complaints while Maddie wasn't there to defend herself, not that Dottie ever hesitated to air her grievances directly to Maddie.

She shook her head and sighed then grabbed her phone, which she'd set down in order to pet Goliath more satisfactorily. It occurred to her that this would be her first call to Nadia. Up to now Maddie had allowed her to take the lead in almost every aspect of their relationship, which was a little odd. Maddie wasn't aggressive by nature, but she usually held her own well enough to strike a nice balance with her partners.

Suddenly inexplicably nervous, Maddie took a deep breath to calm herself, but it didn't work. Instead, her thoughts drifted back to the weirdness of their morning and her uncertainty after Nadia's departure, magnifying her anxiety. If not for her need to figure out who killed Howard, Maddie was sure she would wait all day, possibly even all week, for Nadia to contact her, a thought that startled her. Though she wasn't known for being the aggressor where romance was concerned, passivity wasn't her habit either. She liked to have at least some control, which wasn't an option if she let herself be a wallflower.

Knowing that, she tried to focus on Howard, his murder and her desire to know who was responsible. She owed it to Howard and Goliath—and herself—to find out what had happened and why. Once she was satisfied that a vicious killer was off the streets, then she could focus on self-examination and her assertiveness in her new relationship. Until then, she had a murder to solve. Apparently there was nothing like gory death to calm her nerves—now that she had taken the anticipation of romance out of the conversation, she could think of it more as a business call, and those she was good at.

Without further hesitation, she dialed and waited eagerly for Nadia to pick up, but with every ring her nerves reasserted themselves over her dwindling confidence. After the third ring, an odd blend of disappointment and relief filled her as she prepared to leave a message, but Nadia answered at the last moment.

"You missed me already?" Just the sound of Nadia's voice, low and inviting, turned Maddie's spine to jelly. So much for staying focused on business. She noted with pleasure that Nadia sounded happy to hear from her, a fact that instantly helped her relax.

"I missed you right away, but I'm trying to play hard to get."

"I thought I already got you," Nadia teased.

"You're not wrong," Maddie replied, thrilled at their playful banter. There was no trace of the distance she thought she'd felt this morning. It had probably all been in her head, and it wouldn't be the first time her self-consciousness had made something out of nothing.

"What's up?" Nadia asked, sounding cheerful and lifting Maddie's spirits further. "Or were you just calling to tell me what a great time you had last night and that you can't wait to do it again?"

Maddie reflected on the previous night and smiled, not only because she'd finally resuscitated her sex life (and in a glorious, fireworks and heavenly choir of angels kind of way), but also because she'd had fun. Even on what was possibly the lamest second date in the history of romantic entanglements, they'd both had a good time. She'd enjoyed every moment with Nadia and was starting to let her thoughts drift toward the future.

"I did have a great time, and I really can't wait to do it again," Maddie echoed Nadia's leading question.

"But?" Nadia asked expectantly, and Maddie couldn't decide if it was good or bad thing that Nadia was already reading her so well. She leaned toward good.

"I need a favor."

"I hope it's a fun favor."

Maddie could envision a smoldering look on Nadia's face or at least a wiggling of her eyebrows—she was too big a flirt to let an opportunity like that pass her by. Maddie's stomach did a little flip, and she wished she didn't have to end their play so soon.

"It's probably not, but maybe the 'thank you' will be."

"You're killing me," Nadia groaned. "Whatever it is, I'll do it."

"I need Goliath's veterinary records."

"Why? Is anything wrong?"

Maddie instantly regretted not building up to her request— Nadia sounded panicked, of course. She was an animal lover whose profession exposed her to any number of catastrophes and afflictions that could befall a dog, so who knew where her thoughts would lead? On top of that, she obviously adored Goliath.

"No," Maddie reassured her. "He's fine, sleeping at my feet as we speak."

"Thank goodness." Nadia breathed a sigh of relief. "Why do you want his records?"

"I think there might be information in them that will help me find Howard's murderer."

"You're still looking into that?" Nadia asked, the warmth gone from her voice.

"I am, and I think that his murder had something to do with Goliath. I just don't know what exactly."

Nadia hesitated. "Can we talk about this tonight?"

"Talk about what?" Maddie grew irritated. She couldn't help it. She was close to making a breakthrough, and she had no patience for obstacles. "Either you can give me his records, or you can't. I don't see what there is to discuss."

Nadia didn't answer immediately, but Maddie heard her take a deep breath and release it.

"I hate that you're doing this." She spoke tersely. "I'm worried that something bad will happen to you if you don't stop. And if something bad does happen to you, and I helped put you in danger, I'll never forgive myself."

Maddie's anger softened. How could she be mad at Nadia for wanting to protect her? "I promise you that I will be careful. And the sooner I figure this out, the sooner you won't have to worry about me being in danger. I'll go back to being a boring, mild-mannered, bookish and completely nonthreatening dog walker. What could be safer than that?"

Nadia blew out another deep breath, obviously weighing her options while Maddie waited anxiously for her answer.

Finally she spoke. "All right, you win. I can bring them over tonight. Around six, if that works for you."

"That's perfect. Thank you," Maddie answered, excited to finally be making progress on her investigation. "I'll make you dinner."

"Maybe we'll even get to eat it this time," Nadia joked.

"Anything could happen," Maddie replied, glad to end the call on a less serious note.

Back in her kitchen, Maddie found Dottie in the exact same place she had left her and thought it was entirely possible that she hadn't moved from her seat. She was smiling and petting Bart, whose chin rested on her thigh. He emitted a little satisfied grunt, obviously enjoying the behind-the-ear scratching Dottie, with her expensively manicured fingernails, so thoroughly provided. Maddie smiled as Bart's hind leg began thumping on the floor, and she wouldn't have been surprised if his eyes rolled back in his head. Maybe, since she was the reason Dottie had come over, she would be forgiven for her earlier sin. She doubted that Bart would give her that much credit though.

Maddie also noticed that, though Dottie's glass was full, the pitcher in front of her was completely empty, not even an ice cube remained. Maddie tried to figure out just how much alcohol Dottie had consumed in the relatively short period of time since she'd walked through the door and cursed herself for being heavy-handed with the gin. Maybe she could surreptitiously water down what was left in Dottie's glass, she thought as she pondered the possible ways to bring her friend a little closer to the sober side of life.

"Huevos rancheros," Dottie said, interrupting Maddie's thoughts.

"Excuse me?" Maddie asked, concerned that Dottie was farther gone that she'd originally anticipated.

"That's what I want to eat." She slapped her hand on the table. "Huevos rancheros." She rolled her r's more enthusiastically than a Spanish teacher. She was obviously a little tipsy.

"Are you sure you don't want to just keep saying it?"

"I love saying 'huevos rancheros.'" She added even more flourish to the words. "But it also sounds delicious."

"I don't know how to make huevos rancheros," Maddie said, shaking her head in minor frustration but pleased nonetheless that Dottie was willing to eat.

"Look it up. That's what computers are for."

"Yes, computers exist so that I can cater to your whims." But Maddie searched for a recipe anyway, and to her surprise found one that she thought she could pull off.

"I called Ruth while you were off plotting your elopement."

Maddie shuddered at the mention of her nemesis. She had never actively hated anyone as much as she loathed Ruth Charles.

"She doesn't know Goliath's show name either, not that she was entirely forthcoming once I told her who the information was for. You still haven't contacted her to apologize, have you?"

Maddie grimaced as she gathered ingredients, pretending to be too busy to answer.

"You'll never get any information out of her if you refuse to interact with her. She's not really the type to voluntarily help others."

"I know I have to talk to her," Maddie said, resigned to the inevitably unpleasant task. "There are just other things I'd rather do first, like having root canals on all of my teeth. Without Novocain."

"It can't be any less pleasant to talk to her than it is to run eight thousand miles a day." Maddie threw her a look of extreme irritation, which Dottie ignored. "Just warm up and hit the road, so to speak. Then you'll have your answers, and you'll never have to speak to her again."

"Fine," Maddie sighed. "I'll do it soon. Can you give me her phone number again?" Maddie looked at the recipe to make sure she was properly preparing Dottie's breakfast, and a thought occurred to her. "Give me her address too. Maybe I can write a letter of apology."

"That won't slow down the investigation even the tiniest bit." Dottie didn't even bother to mask her sarcastic tone.

As Maddie set a plate of food and a glass of water in front of her, Dottie asked, "Have you considered what you'll do if the love doctor doesn't have the information you need?"

"You mean other than calling Ruth Charles?"

Dottie nodded as she delicately chewed Maddie's first (and based on Dottie's pleased grin, successful) attempt at huevos rancheros.

"I have no idea."

"I do." Dottie beamed. "It's a long shot, but you might be able to acquire some information from Goliath's breeder."

"If I knew who Goliath's breeder was."

"And if he's a better breeder than Shelly's story indicated."

"What do you mean?" Maddie bit into her own breakfast, pleased with the results.

"Petunia, everything Shelly told us about Howard's epic dog retrieval journey indicates the ignominious, despicable nature of the cretin who manufactured dogs for profit."

Maddie remembered Dottie's incredulity when Shelly Monk had talked about Goliath's appearance in her life. She had never gotten around to asking Dottie about her vehement abhorrence.

"Good breeders, quality breeders have the breeds' best interests in mind. A reputable breeder never would have traded a purebred puppy for a wad of cash and left the buyer to figure it out on his own. They carefully screen potential buyers, provide advice and guidance on the breed and rarely advertise. In other words, pet, they don't do it for the money. They do it out of love and admiration for the breed."

In the past, Maddie would have dismissed the term "responsible breeder" as an oxymoron. There was no way that selfishly and recklessly adding to the pet population could be considered in any way responsible. She had always thought of breeders as money-hungry, soul-sucking bullies and had never even considered giving them the benefit of the doubt. Now, however, she wondered if she'd been too quick to judge.

Knowing Dottie's love for animals, Maddie doubted she would endorse any mistreatment, no matter how in vogue the product. Even taking Dottie's tendency toward willful delusion into consideration, she believed that the welfare of animals would still come first with Dottie, and Maddie felt a bit unsettled by this new picture of the breeding world. Maybe, she thought, just possibly there might be some breeders out there who weren't absolute miscreants. Maybe. Before she surrendered to a thorough reassessment of the breeding world, however, another thought occurred to her.

"If Goliath's breeder was as shady as you think, is it possible that Goliath isn't a purebred?"

"It happens, angel. Looking at Goliath, however, I think it's more likely that he simply lacks proper documentation."

Maddie sat silently for several minutes, staring at Goliath as he snoozed in Bart's dog bed in the corner. What secrets were locked up in his past? "I'm beginning to think that if we figure out the truth about Goliath, everything else will fall into place," she said. "Howard was hiding something about him, and whatever it was got him killed."

CHAPTER TWENTY-THREE

Halfway through her breakfast, Dottie pushed away her plate and declared herself sated and ready to begin her busy day. Maddie doubted that Dottie had any business more pressing to tend to than a massage and a facial, but she kept her suspicions to herself. As she poured her friend into a cab, she promised to call when she unlocked the mystery of Howard's murder with whatever key she discovered in Goliath's veterinary records.

Since Maddie's investigation was on hold until Nadia arrived at six (probably a little longer, if her libido had any say in the matter), she decided to kill a few hours by visiting Granny Doyle and making sure she was settled in back at home. Not that Maddie thought her mother would just drop Granny at her doorstep and be on her way to bigger and better things, but Maddie couldn't help wanting to be certain that Granny Doyle had everything she needed during her recuperation.

As usual, Maddie made the trip to her grandmother's house on foot—it was only six and a half blocks away, and she couldn't justify driving such a short distance on such a lovely day. The sky—a perfect, picturesque blue dotted with fluffy white clouds—reminded her of a child's drawing, and the mild temperature felt like a reward for enduring the heat, humidity and rain of the previous week. It would be a perfect day to throw open all of the windows and enjoy the light, cool breeze rolling off the lake (if all of her windows still opened, she thought with a touch of aggravation). But the day was too gorgeous to stay aggravated for long, and Maddie's thoughts wandered to her grandmother.

While spending time with Granny in any location would have been preferable to the hospital, Granny Doyle's house was one of Maddie's favorite places on the planet. Not only had she spent a large part of her childhood there, exploring all three floors of Granny Doyle's Victorian home until she knew the house as well as she knew her own skin, but just a few years ago she'd lived with Granny for several months while laboring with her father to make her own home habitable.

At first she'd balked at Granny's suggestion that they become "roomies" when Maddie's lease ended before the remodeling did—how awkward and embarrassing to be a grown woman living with her grandmother. In truth, however, it was less crowded and no more uncomfortable than living with her parents. Her only other option was to move in with her girlfriend at the time, and she really didn't want to open that door—the one that led to Cameron standing on Maddie's front porch with all of her possessions once her lease was up. (Of course, the relationship had ended before that became an issue, but how was Maddie to know that was going to happen?)

Living with Granny had worked out so well that Maddie had almost regretted moving to her own place. Not only had they grown even closer in that brief time, but Granny also never resented the nights that Maddie was too exhausted from work and remodeling to do anything but fall into bed. Even though Maddie had tried to show her appreciation by helping out around the house, Granny—too stubborn to ever ask for help—hadn't allowed Maddie to do more than her "fair share." She scolded Maddie whenever she beat Granny to any of the house or yard work.

So Maddie wasn't entirely surprised to find everything— including the lawn—neat and orderly when she arrived. Granny Doyle was habitually tidy (a fact that Maddie held responsible for her own excessive neatness), so Maddie assumed the house had been in pristine condition when Granny got sick. Still, there should have been some evidence of her lengthy absence. After four days in the hospital, even Granny Doyle could fall behind.

At the very least, Maddie had expected to find the grass overgrown. She had planned on struggling to maneuver Granny's old-fashioned push mower through the lush, thick grass of her front and backyards, but someone had beaten her to it. Granny had always been too independent to let anyone else do what she felt she could do herself. One of the few disagreements they'd had during Maddie's stay had been over Granny's stubborn refusal to let her more able-bodied granddaughter care for the lawn versus Maddie's narrow-minded insistence that Granny's age incapacitated her, so Maddie wondered if the freshly trimmed grass was Granny's doing or if someone had taken care of it without Granny's knowledge or permission. Maddie hoped it was the latter and that Granny wouldn't argue about taking that responsibility back on.

When Granny opened the door for Maddie, Maddie was taken aback by Granny's appearance. Though Maddie knew that her illness had been serious and tiring, she had expected Granny's liberation from the hospital to be more rejuvenating. Instead, she looked almost as pale and fatigued as she had in the hospital, and there were bruises on her arms where the IVs had been. She seemed ready to drop as she stepped aside to let her youngest granddaughter in, and it broke Maddie's heart to see how feeble Granny had become. But their hug lasted for several moments, and Maddie was relieved both by the lack of tubes, wires and IVs obstructing the hug and by the strength she could feel in her grandmother's embrace. She wasn't so feeble after all.

She also was obviously enjoying the comforts of her own home. She had recently showered, and it was nice to see her in an outfit that didn't tie at the back. However, Granny hadn't bothered to style her hair after she'd washed it, which was unusual. Granny wasn't one of those old ladies who enjoyed getting her hair set at weekly salon appointments, preferring instead the simplicity of a braid to keep it out of her way. She said that if it worked for Jane Goodall, it was good enough for her. Now it hung loose around her shoulders, shifting slightly in the gentle breeze coming through the open windows.

"Shouldn't you be resting, Granny?"

"Nonsense. I've been resting for four days. I'm sick of resting."

"Don't tell me you felt up to mowing your lawn. I was going to take care of that for you."

Granny poured them both some iced tea and ordered Maddie to sit. "Mrs. Harkin had her grandson tend to my yard work while I was being held hostage by the AMA. I told her to send him by tomorrow so I can pay him. She told me it wasn't necessary, but he did good work. He deserves to be paid." Maddie smiled at her grandmother's ever-present sense of fairness. "I think I'll bake him some cookies too."

"If you need any help baking—"

"Forget it," Granny cut her off. "You just want to get your hands on my oatmeal cookie recipe, and I'll have to get a lot closer to the grave before I hand that over."

Maddie felt her grandmother's offhanded comment like a punch in the gut. Though Granny had insisted throughout her hospitalization that she'd never been seriously ill, Maddie had been terrified that she'd lose her. Once her condition had been stabilized, Maddie had let herself believe that life would return to normal, with her grandmother a constant presence and one of her best friends. She realized now that she'd taken Granny's release from the hospital as a sign that she would be around forever, a sort of "all clear" for her future health, which was a ridiculous thought. As Granny's joke reminded her, she wouldn't live forever. Sometimes Maddie marveled at how her brain worked, or failed to, as in this case.

Maddie felt her throat constricting as tears welled in her eyes.

Granny must have noticed her granddaughter's emotional distress because she admonished Maddie. "Don't start writing my eulogy yet, child. I've got a lot of living yet to do, and it'll take more than some temperamental blood pressure to do me in." She squeezed Maddie's hand reassuringly then said, "And that's the last I'm going to say about my health. The door to that subject is officially closed."

The corners of Maddie's mouth twitched up in a weak smile, and she wiped her eyes. Shaking off her bleak thoughts, she steered the conversation back to lighter matters. "Wouldn't you like it if someone made you cookies once in a while?" she asked around the persistent lump in her throat.

"Cookies taste better when you make them for other people," Granny countered. "It's the joy of baking."

"So you want to deprive me of joy?" Maddie teased. The more she played with her grandmother, the better she felt, and the better Granny looked—some color was returning to her cheeks already, and there was a mischievous gleam in her eye.

"You have plenty of other sources of joy," Granny said. "Speaking of which, how are things going with your new lady friend?"

"Smooth transition, Granny."

"You don't live as long as I have without learning some tricks, like when someone is trying to avoid the question."

Maddie smiled more fully at her grandmother. Even though she and Granny had an unconventional relationship, she couldn't see herself sharing the intimate details of her relationship with Nadia. She didn't even want to share those with Dottie (though Dottie made sure she didn't have much choice in the matter). Still, she knew she had to answer Granny's question.

"It's going well." Maddie didn't elaborate, but she couldn't help the smile that spread across her face as her stomach fluttered with the now familiar and not unpleasant nervousness at the thought of Nadia.

"I see," Granny said, and Maddie took a drink of her tea to hide the blush she knew was creeping across her face. "Is she a good kisser?"

Maddie almost choked on her tea. "Granny!" Maddie shrieked.

"Don't act shocked," Granny said. "You didn't think I ended up having four kids without learning the value of a good kiss, did you?"

Maddie had never thought about it at all and allowed her red face and horrified expression to say as much. She no more wanted to talk about Nadia than Granny wanted to talk about her health, but it certainly seemed preferable to a discussion of her grandparents' sex life. Just the idea of taking a trip down that particular branch of memory lane made Maddie wish a hole would open up and swallow her.

"I like her a lot, Granny." Maddie pretended the subject of kissing never came up.

"That must be why you look like the government just outlawed puppies." Maddie had never been able to hide anything from her grandmother, apparently not even after a four-day hospitalization that should have exhausted her and dulled her observational skills. "What's the problem, Matilda?"

Maddie studied her fingernails, avoiding Granny's persistent gaze for a full minute before she broke. "She makes me nervous. She's beautiful and smart and cares about animals, and apparently I've entered some kid of bizarro world where perfect women are available and attracted to me. I don't understand it at all."

Granny's face took on a serious, dour expression. "You're a homeowner and a successful business woman, and you happen to be the spitting image of your grandmother when she was your age, and you don't understand what women see in you," Granny huffed, and Maddie realized too late that she'd offended her grandmother. "I'll never understand how someone so smart can be so foolish."

Maddie knew she resembled her grandmother. She'd heard it all her life, but she'd always disregarded those comparisons since they were only free-flowing when Maddie was down on herself. Not once had anyone commented on her resemblance to Granny when Maddie was feeling good about herself. Even when she looked at old pictures of Granny, she didn't see more than a passing similarity, probably because the pictures of her grandmother showed a beautiful, poised woman, nothing like

Maddie felt, and their physical similarities did not make up for the differences in their personalities.

"If I'm such a catch," Maddie asked quietly, "why has everybody let me go?"

"Think about the past for a minute, child. Did you really want to be caught by any of those buffoons?"

Maddie didn't want to dwell on her romantic failures, but a cursory glance at her dating history confirmed Granny's assertion—Maddie's past was littered with the corpses of relationships she was, with her twenty-twenty hindsight, glad to be free of.

Granny seemed to sense Maddie's reluctance to dissect her past romantic entanglements. She refilled their tea. "When do you see her again?" she asked.

"Tonight. She's coming over for dinner."

"A second date so quick. She moves fast," Granny said, sounding impressed.

You have no idea, thought Maddie. She said, "Third date, actually."

Granny's eyebrows raised in surprise. "Three dates in three days. What are you worried about?"

"I did tell her I'd cook for her."

Granny laughed. "Why don't I help you make something for dessert?" she said. "Then the night won't be a complete disaster."

"Thanks Granny." Maddie hugged her grandmother once more before they began searching through Granny's recipes.

CHAPTER TWENTY-FOUR

Thanks to her dad's vast experience building and remodeling homes, Maddie had ended up with a kitchen that a gourmet chef would envy. Not only had he ensured that the layout provided ample counter, cabinet and floor space, but he'd also set her up with high-end appliances, some of which she knew she didn't have the skills to justify owning and never would. Most of the time she was preparing food for one, and she rarely made herself anything more elaborate than a salad or a microwave dinner. What use did she have for a Wolf range or a Sub-Zero built-in refrigerator? But her father had insisted that it would increase the resale value of the house and suggested that, with the right equipment, she might learn to love cooking. Maddie suspected that her dad hoped her skills would rise to the level of her equipment, and this was his attempt to secure a family chef other than Granny Doyle. So far it hadn't worked.

Even armed with all of that technology and Granny's apple pie for dessert, Maddie figured her best hope for a successful meal would be that staple of summer dining—a barbecue. With the mild temperatures, gentle breeze and clear sky, it was the perfect day to fire up the grill. Maddie knew Nadia wasn't a vegetarian—she'd ordered maple-glazed pork chops on their first date and had seemed content with pepperoni pizza the next night. Maddie figured she'd probably be safe throwing a couple of steaks on the grill.

That meant she needed to go back to the store to get steaks. And maybe some vegetables. Or potatoes. What good, at least partially Irish woman didn't like potatoes? Maddie threw together a quick grocery list; she knew it was overboard, but obsessing over food helped to keep her mind distracted. In just under four hours, Nadia would arrive with information that could uncover the truth about Howard's death. If she thought about it too much, she became impatient and agitated.

At the store she panicked. What if Nadia didn't eat steak? She grabbed some chicken breasts. But what if pigs were the only animals Nadia ate? Maddie tossed pork chops and pork tenderloin into her cart, which was already overflowing with the mounds of produce she'd selected (potatoes, asparagus, tomatoes, three kinds of lettuce, summer squash, corn on the cob, cucumbers and an array of fruits and berries) just to be sure she'd have something Nadia would like. As she careened toward the liquor department, another worry descended upon her. What would Nadia want to drink? She'd had wine on Friday, and they'd never gotten around to drinks last night. What if Nadia didn't drink beer or hard liquor, both of which Maddie had in excess? She added a few bottles of wine to her rapidly filling cart.

Eventually Maddie made it out of the grocery store with enough food and booze to host a week-long picnic for all of her employees and their closest friends. But she was still on edge, not only about Nadia but also about pinning her hopes on the insights she could provide. Nadia might not even have any information related to Goliath's dog show victory. After all, Goliath's victory had been in Colorado (if, in fact, he had won a dog show at all). Nadia might not have been his doctor at that point, and even if she did have those details, there was no guarantee they'd help. This line of thinking was all a hunch. Howard's murder might be completely unrelated to dogs and dog shows, and Goliath, like Maddie, might be an innocent bystander, his life irrevocably altered by one cruel and bewildering act. At this point, the best she could hope for was that some answers could be found in Goliath's past.

By the time Nadia showed up (fifteen minutes late, not that Maddie was watching the clock or growing exponentially more impatient with every second that passed), Maddie had taken the boys on a long walk (during which Bart showed signs that he'd forgotten his bath time grudge), showered again and fretted over what to wear. Ultimately, she decided that since Nadia still seemed to like her even after seeing her at her most casual and least polished, she could get away with jeans and a navy blue cami that she could throw a shirt over later if necessary.

Clean, dressed and left with nothing else to obsess over, Maddie turned her attention to the food. While she kept an eye on the clock, she prepared macaroni and cheese (not from a box), roasted potato salad, coleslaw and a tossed salad. She opted to skip the corn on the cob (not the most attractive dining experience) and the baked beans (for obvious reasons), even though she had been certain in the store that both were a good idea.

Throughout the day—on her way to Granny's or the store, on a walk with the dogs or peering outside to see if Nadia was early, or right on time, or just a little late—she had noticed a surplus of cops, on bikes and in cars, patrolling her neighborhood. She didn't know if she was more aware of them because of her recent encounters with law enforcement or if Officer Murphy had made good on her promise to keep an eye on her. Either way, she felt better knowing they were so omnipresent. It hardly seemed likely that Howard's killer would attack her or cause more damage to her home when there were so many cops roaming the streets.

When she opened the door to (finally) let Nadia in, a police car drove past her house and slowed down. Maddie thought that it might have been Officer Murphy behind the wheel, but she didn't spend enough time looking to be sure. She was distracted by the woman on her front porch, who, as usual, looked better than any mortal woman had a right to look.

Maddie couldn't help but notice the fit of Nadia's jeans, the scenic view created by the vee of her T-shirt and her shampoo commercial-quality hair. Didn't she ever have a frumpy day? Maddie realized that she would have to put more effort into her appearance if she didn't want to look out of place next to Nadia.

Maddie also noticed that Nadia had come to the door empty-handed. She hoped Nadia hadn't forgotten to bring Goliath's records (maybe she left them in the car?), but that question couldn't be the first thing out of Maddie's mouth. No matter how eager she was to make some headway in her investigation, she didn't really want Nadia to think that veterinary records were the only reason Maddie was eager to see her. To that end, she offered Nadia an ardent welcome before they even made it through the door.

"If your greetings are always this good, it almost makes leaving worthwhile."

Maddie smiled and led Nadia and both dogs, who weren't even trying to contain their excitement, to the kitchen where a profusion of side dishes (some of which could be considered entrees) crowded the countertops. She was about to ask Nadia which of the several available meat options she'd prefer when Nadia spoke.

"I know no one's ever going to mistake me for a runway model, but how much did you think I'd eat?" She sounded both surprised and playful.

Maddie grinned. "Maybe I just wanted to make sure you keep your curves."

"No worries there. If the past is any indication of the future, they're not going anywhere."

Maddie smiled at Nadia. "I wasn't sure what you'd like," she said, "so I thought options would be the best way to go."

"And then you decided to open an Old Country Buffet in your kitchen? This is an insane amount of food."

Aside from a raised eyebrow, Maddie ignored the Old Country Buffet comment. Her cooking was slightly better than that. "It doesn't even come close to your beverage options," Maddie said.

A short while later, they were outside discussing the day. While the dogs lounged at her feet, Nadia occasionally sipped her beer, and Maddie tended to the grill. Thoroughly absorbed by this picture perfect domestic scene, she almost missed Nadia's confession that she hadn't brought Goliath's records.

"What?" Maddie couldn't hide her irritation.

"I know I promised I would give them to you, but there's a lot of information. Howard really wasn't hesitant to bring Goliath into the office."

"Okay." Still irritated, Maddie focused her attention on the chicken breasts she was grilling. She'd let them marinate in a teriyaki barbecue sauce. It had sounded delicious when she found the recipe. She didn't want to burn their dinner simply because she got distracted by her disappointment.

"I thought you could tell me what you're looking for, and I could weed through the proliferation of information in Goliath's history and just give you what would be useful."

Maddie tore her attention away from the chicken to smile at Nadia. She had to agree that sounded helpful.

"That is unless—"

Maddie's smile disappeared. "Unless what?"

"Unless I can talk you out of this." Nadia had the sense to look sheepish as she spoke.

"You can't, and I'm not sure why you're so opposed to me looking into this."

"I'm concerned about your safety."

"What makes you think I'm in any danger?"

"Among other things, I doubt that a person who beats an old man to death would just throw up his hands and say, 'I guess I'll let you take me to the cops now' when you show up armed with whatever evidence you think is hiding in Goliath's records."

"I'm not going to try to…citizen's arrest anyone. I'm not a vigilante. I just want to know the truth." The chicken smoldering on the grill was effectively forgotten as Maddie went on the defensive. "What makes you think I wouldn't tell the police what I learn?"

"How much have you told them so far?"

"Everything!" Maddie practically barked her answer, like she was winning a presidential debate with that one word.

"Really?" Nadia seemed surprised. "When did you do that?"

Maddie opened her mouth, then realized how damning her answer would be. She sat beside Nadia and softly said, "Yesterday. After the brick came through my window." She hoped that perhaps the lie of omission in her description of an autonomous brick would go unnoticed. It didn't.

"Because you think the killer threw the brick?"

Maddie nodded, aware she had dug a hole for herself.

"It's not so crazy that I'm worried about you, is it?"

Maddie offered a meek "No." But she wasn't willing to give up on figuring out who had turned her life so completely upside down, and she didn't think she'd ever felt as strongly about anything as she did about Goliath's history somehow being linked to Howard's death. She held Nadia's hand.

"I promise you that if anything in Goliath's records suggests who the killer might be, I will give that information to the police immediately." She looked into Nadia's eyes. "I don't want to get hurt, and I don't want to put myself in danger. This isn't some kind of adventure for me. I'm not thrill-seeking here. I just want to know what happened to my friend."

Nadia remained silent long enough for Maddie to notice the smoke billowing out of the grill and realize she'd ruined their dinner. Pulling the charred remains of their meal off the grill and wondering if the dogs would eat chicken when it more closely resembled charcoal than food, Maddie heard Nadia speak. "All right. Tell me what you're looking for, and I'll get it to you tomorrow."

"Thank you," Maddie said and offered Nadia an incredibly grateful kiss. "I hope you don't mind," she said as she settled herself on Nadia's lap, "but we're having steak for dinner."

CHAPTER TWENTY-FIVE

Maddie drove to work in the morning. She hated driving such a short distance and, as a rule, tried to walk whenever possible, but travelling on foot was simply not an option. For one thing, she had the equivalent of a fallout shelter's stockpile of food to carry with her. Even if she ate nothing but the remains of last night's dinner every day for the next week, Maddie doubted she would ever consume all that was left over. She hated to let the food go to waste and knew her employees would appreciate it.

It was also the first day of her trial week with Alphonse (assuming Adam didn't run her off the property when she showed up at his door that afternoon). Since she was trying to impress Alphonse's dads, she wanted to be even more punctual than usual, and the commute to Evanston was too much to undertake as a pedestrian. It would be better to have her car on hand when she needed to head north.

On top of all that, she'd gotten a late start that morning. Even though Nadia had left before seven, the disruption of her first "school night" adult sleepover in years had delayed her more than she'd anticipated. She hadn't gotten a chance to run (which was probably for the best since the cut on her foot was still a little tender), and she barely made it to her desk before Patrick came through the door offering a broad smile and a cheery hello, sure indicators that he'd had a good weekend.

Normally, Maddie would have matched or surpassed his good mood. Unlike most of the working world, she didn't view Monday mornings with dread. She loved her work. How could she not when, usually, the hardest part of her day was resisting the pleading of sad puppy eyes for a little more time outside or not to be put back in the crate? Beyond that, she worked with great people. She'd somehow managed to hire a collection of creative, compassionate animal lovers who were fun to be around. She didn't socialize much with her employees, as it made the infrequent calls for discipline more difficult than they already were, but she got along so well with most of them that, when they finally left her company for other pursuits, she would gladly stay in contact with them.

This, however, was not a typical Monday. In addition to the uncertainty of her future as Alphonse's walker, she also had to find a way to distract herself for the entire day until she could get her hands on Goliath's records. She had preoccupied herself on Sunday with excessive food prep. She didn't have that option today, and as much as she loved the animals she worked with, she knew that their lack of conversational skills meant that her unengaged mind would dwell on whatever thoughts popped into it. Lately, those thoughts fell into three categories: Granny, Howard and Nadia. With Granny now in the clear, it was going to be a long day of dodging her persistent curiosity about Howard while also distracting herself from her lingering doubts about Nadia.

In hopes of significantly reducing her wait time, Maddie had offered to drop by Nadia's office in the afternoon to pick up the pertinent parts of Goliath's records. That way she could peruse everything before Nadia finished work, and then they would have the rest of the night to themselves (unless, of course, Maddie managed to solve the crime and was busy telling Fitzwilliam what she knew while deflecting the inevitable castigation for butting in).

"Have I worn out my welcome already?" Nadia asked, and when Maddie's only response was a confused look, she added, "That was my excuse for coming over again tonight."

"I thought *I* was your excuse."

"You are, but you're also a distraction. A very pleasant one, not that that would make a difference to my clients." Nadia kissed her. "It would be better if you didn't come by."

She should have been pleased by the compliment, but Maddie's first thought was that Nadia was being evasive and again trying to discourage the investigation by stalling it. Her irritation decreased, however, when Nadia pointed out how long it might take her to sort through Goliath's overflowing records for the information Maddie wanted.

Thinking that the key to Howard's death probably had nothing to do with run-of-the-mill veterinary visits, Maddie initially asked Nadia to give her any information she had related to dog shows. Almost immediately, though, she amended her request to include anything that involved another dog or a person other than Howard. If Goliath was the key to all of this, Maddie doubted it was because of his mere existence or innocuous events like vaccinations or expressed anal glands. She suspected that, somewhere along the line, some interaction between Goliath and someone else had caused a problem. Finding that problem might lead her to finding Howard's killer.

This was all a giant leap of faith, of course, but assuming that this, the latest in a long line of hunches, was correct (and assuming that Nadia came up with anything in her search through Goliath's voluminous medical history), Maddie might find some answers as early as tonight. What time tonight, exactly, she wasn't certain, as Nadia had been dodgy about when she might make it to Maddie's house. Maddie understood that a veterinarian didn't have a set quitting time, no matter what the hours posted on her door might say, but she found the various delays and vague answers from Nadia disquieting. She didn't want to have doubts about a woman for whom she was developing strong feelings, but she was perplexed about

Nadia's caginess. She wasn't entirely sure she wanted to know the answer.

For the most part, she managed to steer clear of that line of thought throughout the morning, thanks, in large part, to the other concern running roughshod over her mental and emotional well-being—her impending encounter with Adam Whelan. She did not fare well in her attempts to ignore the knot that settled in her stomach every time she considered what might be waiting for her in Evanston, and when she arrived at Alphonse's house in the early afternoon, her tendency to expect the worst overwhelmed her. She thought for a moment that she might vomit.

After a brief delay, Maddie's anxiety disappeared almost entirely. When Adam opened the door, he greeted her warmly. He ushered her inside and offered her a drink, as though he had forgotten that she was there on a business, rather than a social, call. Maddie was momentarily confused by his graciousness. Had he not witnessed the hostility at their last encounter? She knew she hadn't imagined the tension between Albert and herself, and so wondered how Adam could seem so blithe and chipper in the face of someone who had, in essence, accused him of murder. Maybe Adam was a conflict avoider. If that was the case, it made him a much less viable suspect for a brutal murder. Or, he might be a sociopath, in which case she was probably already screwed, no matter what she did.

Interrupting Maddie's thoughts, Adam handed over Alphonse's leash and reminded her of his Walking Protocol: the walk should last twenty to twenty-five minutes and should, under no circumstances, include rolling around in the grass or frolicking with other dogs, as these activities could be a metaphorical stick of dynamite to Alphonse's show readiness. Further, Alphonse should sit before crossing any streets, and he was to heel unless relieving himself.

Nodding, Maddie prepared to embark upon the least-fun dog walk she'd ever taken.

"Be a good boy, Alphonse," Adam spoke in a surprisingly indulgent tone before closing the door behind Maddie and her new dog friend.

As they made their way around the neighborhood—via a route that Alphonse seemed to have laid out in advance—Maddie was pleased to see that Alphonse, despite his restrictions, found ways to enjoy his time outdoors. He barked hello to every dog they saw, solicited petting from several passersby and sniffed a handful of flowers in the various gardens they passed. His tail wagged joyfully almost the entire twenty-three minutes and seventeen seconds that they were gone.

She was also amazed by his exceptional behavior. She never had to command him to sit or remind him to heel. He checked in with her regularly as they strolled around the neighborhood and didn't kick massive clumps of dirt and grass in her direction after he finished taking care of business. He was, without a doubt, the most well-trained dog she had ever met, and she reflected once again on the behavioral differences between Goliath and Alphonse (or almost any other dog). Goliath's obvious lack of training was glaring in comparison to Alphonse, and Maddie again questioned the likelihood that Goliath had won a dog show. She found it increasingly difficult to believe that Goliath's victory existed anywhere outside of Howard's version of reality.

She stopped herself before she got too wrapped up in those thoughts. For one thing, she was supposed to be focused on Alphonse (though it seemed entirely possible that he would be fine walking himself, waste disposal included). For another, she wouldn't begin to have answers to those questions until tonight, and the idea of torturing herself for the next several hours contained not the slightest appeal.

When she returned Alphonse in one joyful, still remarkably well-groomed piece, Adam's lavish thanks seemed heartfelt, and they both continued to ignore the accusatory elephant in the room. Adam even gushed about his relief at having Maddie on the job. "We've been desperate to find someone good enough for our little boy," he said, beaming at her.

She'd murmured her perplexed appreciation and then fled before he could remember that they were sort of enemies.

Back at the office after her final walk of the day, Maddie, momentarily alone and out of excuses, quit stalling and finally called to apologize to Ruth Charles. Ruth hung up as soon as Maddie identified herself.

"At least I tried," she muttered.

Deciding not to make a nuisance of herself, Maddie set aside the phone number and address that Dottie had given her. Maybe later, she thought, she would write Ruth an apology. Much, much later. She hadn't noticed before that Ruth lived in her neighborhood, and after briefly considering how much of a hassle it would be to move to a completely different neighborhood, she went back to work and managed to stay focused on her business for almost all of the time before the last of her walkers returned. She was in a good place, businesswise, when she left for the day.

At home with little to distract her until Nadia arrived, Maddie grew impatient. The boys weren't much help—they conked out after a lengthy walk and a vigorous game of fetch, leaving Maddie alone to stare down the next couple of hours. Her contemplation of sock drawer reorganization was thwarted by her phone.

"Well?" Dottie's impatience was palpable. "What's the verdict?"

"On?"

Dottie's exasperated sigh resonated for several seconds before she explained. "Your *raison d'être* for the last week. Who killed Howard?"

Too late, Maddie realized that she had neglected to call Dottie as promised. "I don't know yet," she answered and explained the delay.

"And now you're wondering about the doctor's motives."

"Yes," Maddie agreed. Considering her typical level of self-absorption, Dottie could be astoundingly perceptive.

"Ask her."

"Of course. I'll just casually inquire if the reason she's reluctant to help me is because she doesn't want me to find out that she's the killer. And if she tries to kill me, I'll have my answer."

"Don't be ludicrous, sunshine. Ask her who she thinks the killer is and pay attention to how she answers. Honestly, pumpkin, I don't know how you expect to become a super sleuth when you don't even know the basics."

"Thank goodness I have you to keep me on track," Maddie answered, avoiding any discussion of her future as a detective.

They spent a few more minutes discussing Granny's health and Dottie's love life before Dottie let Maddie go. She hadn't berated Maddie for forgetting to call and had only elicited two promises for information once Maddie had it, so Maddie assumed Dottie had other, more enticing things to think about and prepared herself for the possibility of another bridesmaid's dress in her near future.

Maddie assumed that she would feel better once Nadia arrived. Her anticipation and worry, she hoped, would come to a blessed end when she got her hands on Goliath's records and she could quell the disquieting doubts about Nadia, but when she finally showed up, Nadia's expression—one of terror and anxiety—made Maddie feel decidedly worse. Without asking, she poured Nadia some wine and tried to subdue her own anxiety as Nadia downed half the glass.

"Thank you." She clutched nervously at a manila folder. "Before I give this to you," she waved the folder in the air and ran her free hand nervously through her hair. "I—I have a confession to make."

CHAPTER TWENTY-SIX

"A confession?" Maddie asked warily.

She felt conflicted by a swarm of emotions. Her initial bewilderment gave way to fleeting joy that she'd inadvertently solved the case. These were followed by shame at the thought that she'd been sleeping with a killer, and then sorrow and embarrassment that Nadia had only pursued her to prevent her from figuring out the truth. "I knew she was too good to be true," Maddie thought, as terror settled upon her.

Meanwhile, without even thinking, she began inching away. If Nadia was about to tell her that she had killed Howard, Maddie needed to put some space between them—even though there weren't any useful weapons nearby, she still didn't want to be within swinging range. Nor did she want to risk angering Nadia with any sudden movements, so she moved slowly, trying not to draw attention to her subtle migration. She made it only a few inches before Nadia grabbed her hand and led her to the couch.

Sitting beside Nadia and hoping desperately that she'd horribly misjudged her, Maddie was torn between the desire for an explanation and a drink. Seeing as it would give her a handy excuse to put herself back at a safe distance, she made the drink offer to Nadia.

"More wine?" she asked and rose to head back into the kitchen.

"Yes." Nadia sounded eager but immediately changed her mind. She hadn't let go of Maddie's hand, and now pulled her gently back. "Can it wait? If I don't say this now, I might lose my nerve."

Maddie sank back down on the couch, and her eyes met Nadia's. She looked more terrified and vulnerable than menacing, and Maddie began to doubt that Nadia could be on the verge of a murder confession. Reflecting on their brief history, Maddie considered how much more evidence was stacked in the "Nadia is a kind and compassionate woman" column than in the "Nadia is a cold-blooded killer of helpless elderly men" column. Well aware of the giant mistake she might be about to make, Maddie ignored her fear and let her guard down.

"Whatever it is, just tell me." She touched Nadia's cheek and offered what she hoped was a reassuring smile.

After a deep breath, Nadia spoke. "When I told you that I helped Howard breed Goliath, I didn't tell you everything."

"What did you leave out?" Maddie tried to speak gently, but she was rapidly losing what little patience she'd had to begin with.

"Goliath isn't a purebred, not in the AKC sense."

"What!" Even though she and Dottie had discussed this possibility, Maddie had never really believed that Goliath could be anything other than a purebred dog. It didn't seem possible. "Then how—" Maddie stopped. She didn't even know how to sort through the jumble of confusion in her brain to formulate any worthwhile questions.

"We tested his DNA. Of course, mistakes can happen, and there's always room for errors or inaccuracies, but there is no doubt in my mind that Goliath is a Great Dane—*all* Great

Dane. He just doesn't come from an established bloodline. His parents weren't registered with the AKC, and neither was his litter. It doesn't make him any less a Great Dane, but it does make him less, um, bankable."

"So that's what you meant when you said that you helped Howard with Goliath's paperwork." Unable to hide her irritation any longer, Maddie strode to the kitchen and poured two healthy servings of bourbon—wine was not going to cut it. After downing her drink, she handed the other to Nadia, who had followed her.

"Sort of." Nadia set her glass down without even taking a sip. "I eliminated any questions Howard might have had about Goliath's genetic makeup, but that was the extent of my involvement. I don't know where he went or how he managed to get papers for Goliath, and I never asked. I didn't want to know."

"But you knew they were fake."

"Yes." Nadia suddenly seemed fascinated with her drink and wouldn't look at anything but her glass. "And I never told anyone, not even the owners who bred their dogs with Goliath. I kept that secret to myself. Until now."

"And what inspired this sudden burst of honesty?"

"You." She looked at Maddie. "You were so determined to find Howard's killer, and when you began to suspect a connection between his death and Goliath—"

"That's why you tried to stop me." Growing angrier by the second, Maddie poured herself another drink.

"I knew I had to tell you. If you were going to find out—and it seemed more and more likely that you would—I wanted it to come from me, but I was too afraid and ashamed. I hoped I could convince you to let the police handle it." She sipped at her drink, her expression vacant. "I can't believe what a fool I was. When Howard gave me the car, he said it was a thank-you, but really he was—"

"Buying your silence?" Maddie knew her voice was harsh, possibly harsher than necessary. She had no idea what had led Nadia to this sequence of astoundingly bad decision-making.

She should reserve judgment until she heard the whole story (or as much of it as Nadia revealed), but reining in her anger seemed nearly impossible at the moment.

"And my integrity." Nadia hung her head. "That's why I refused to take it at first and why I insisted on making payments. Howard hated that I wouldn't take it outright, but I thought I could buy back my honor somehow." She laughed bitterly. "But now…"

"Now Howard is dead."

"I don't know if this had anything to do with his murder—I can't believe anyone would get that angry over breeding."

"You obviously haven't spent much time with the dog show crowd." Maddie reflected on her only real exposure to dog show devotees other than Dottie. It was possible that Dottie's friends represented an extreme and skewed representation of the dog show set, but that strange and bizarrely impassioned group was Maddie's only frame of reference. Based on her experience with them, she had no plans to increase her exposure and no doubt that their obsession over breeding could lead to murder.

"But if it does—" Nadia's voice was strained, and tears gathered in her eyes. "If Howard died because I helped him lie about Goliath, then I'm at least partially responsible for his death, and I don't know if I can live with myself."

Nadia sank to the floor, her breath coming in ragged gasps as she wept. No matter how irresponsible Nadia's behavior had been, she hadn't acted maliciously or set out to hurt anyone. She just hadn't fully considered the consequences of her actions, and she didn't deserve to be in so much pain.

"Listen to me." Maddie gathered her in her arms. "The only person responsible is the one who killed him. Was that you?"

"No!" Seemingly horrified by that suggestion, Nadia recoiled. "I could never do something like that!"

Her emphatic denial rang true, but Maddie realized she could be lying.

Ignoring rationality, Maddie placed a gentle kiss on Nadia's flushed and tear-streaked cheek. "I believe you," she said. Nadia clung tightly to her and launched into an even more vigorous bout of sobbing, her cries of "Poor Howard" and "What have I done?" muffled slightly by Maddie's shoulder.

"Stop beating yourself up over this. We don't even know if Howard's death had anything to do with Goliath's questionable background." But even as she said it, Maddie felt more certain than before that there was a connection.

Later that night, as she held the finally sleeping Nadia in her arms, and the dogs, who had been distant but concerned during Nadia's breakdown, lay snoring in their beds, Maddie's mind raced. All of her earlier doubts, now louder and more persistent, returned. Nadia clearly had a motive to kill Howard. Not only did she regret her actions, but she also resented the hold he had over her. Paying him back was no guarantee that he wouldn't reveal her questionable actions down the road. If he'd wanted to, Howard could have used her past indiscretion to secure future misconduct. But the less cynical side of Maddie's mind refused to accept that possibility. She felt, more than she knew, that Nadia was telling the truth, that she could never kill anyone.

She knew that believing Nadia's claim of innocence, especially when it came immediately after her admission of a significant and long-term lie, could be an epic mistake. It was entirely possible that Nadia's emotional outburst had been an act designed to win Maddie's sympathy and throw her investigation off, again. If so, it was working.

Maddie couldn't reconcile Nadia's anguished sobs with the idea that she was nothing more than a manipulative killer. Her suffering had been too raw to be an act. It had taken Maddie over an hour to calm Nadia enough to coax her off the kitchen floor and into bed, where she'd held her for another hour until her tears subsided, her breathing slowed and she fell into a fitful sleep. Maddie doubted that even Meryl Streep could put on a performance that convincing.

And now Maddie couldn't sleep. As if the nagging question of Nadia's guilt or innocence wasn't enough to keep sleep at bay, there was also the file of potentially mystery-solving paperwork sitting on her kitchen counter, calling to her like a siren. She hadn't had a chance to look at it before Nadia's confession, and it wasn't like she could interrupt Nadia's meltdown to examine the file. All of her attention had been on Nadia and her story.

But now, as Nadia slept, Maddie itched to get her hands on the information—it called to her so intensely that she thought it must be glowing like a beacon in her kitchen. She wasn't sleeping anyway, and inspecting the file seemed like a better use of her time and mental powers than wavering between belief in Nadia's guilt or innocence. She shifted in bed, trying to tug her arm out from under the woman sleeping soundly, if not peacefully, in her embrace, but as soon as she moved, Nadia woke enough to pull both of Maddie's arms around her. She clung to Maddie's left hand with her right, her grip loosening only slightly as she drifted back to sleep.

And there Maddie lay, held prisoner in her bed by a beautiful woman. It was a peculiar and oddly frustrating dilemma, and one that Maddie never suspected she would be faced with. She never dreamed that she'd have a woman this gorgeous in her bed, but now that she did, it seemed absurd that she was thinking about leaving her there to go pore over the medical history of her foster dog.

Though part of her desire to escape was her need to examine the information that Nadia had finally given her, the remainder of her restlessness was due to her uncertainty about her feelings for Nadia. Maddie was sure that they had been progressing toward something more than sex and the occasional meal, but now she didn't know what to think or feel about Nadia's possible connection to Howard's death. She didn't blame Nadia. Obviously, if Nadia had predicted this as the outcome of her dishonesty, she wouldn't have made the same choices. At least, Maddie didn't think she would.

But that nagging doubt was a big stumbling block, and right now, Maddie didn't know if she could overlook it.

CHAPTER TWENTY-SEVEN

Maddie had to wait until after work the following day to get her hands on the information in Goliath's files. They'd gotten a late start in the morning—in all of the turmoil the night before, Maddie had forgotten to set her alarm, and since she hadn't gotten to sleep until well after one, she didn't even stir at her regular waking time. If not for the dogs fussing to go outside, Maddie doubted she would have woken up before she was due at Little Guys.

Maddie had been too flustered by the prospect of tardiness to even think about the file, but after she and Nadia rushed out the door, Maddie regretted not bringing it with her, even though she knew she was better off having left it behind. She wouldn't have an inordinate amount of time during the day to examine the information (it wasn't like she was overwhelmed with downtime at work). If it was with her and she still couldn't concentrate on it, she knew that she'd be obsessing over its useless proximity instead of focusing on her dogs. That, or she wouldn't be able to resist temptation at all. She'd squeeze in occasional glances at every possible moment, and her distraction and frustration would still get the better of her. So she left the file exactly where Nadia had put it before her guilt-fueled meltdown.

Almost the first thing Maddie did when she got home, however, was grab the file and let the dogs into the yard while she read. They would probably have preferred a walk around the neighborhood. They both enjoyed roaming their streets in search of all the good sniffs they could find, greeting their human and canine friends and chasing the bold squirrels who taunted them. The boys didn't ask for much, and they deserved to have whatever would make them feel contented, but for now there was no way Maddie would survive further delay. They would have to satisfy themselves with the amusements in their private playground.

So she refilled their outside water bowl and grabbed some water for herself, and then she settled down to gain some insights on Goliath and, hopefully, find Howard's killer. At first, Maddie struggled to make sense of what she was looking at, both because Nadia's notes were handwritten in penmanship as sloppy and difficult to decipher as one would expect a doctor's handwriting to be, and because everything was abbreviated or written in some sort of veterinary cryptography. Initially she wondered if this had been another of Nadia's stalling tactics, before she'd decided to admit to her role in Howard's grand deception, but she decided to give Nadia the benefit of the doubt. Nadia was a busy woman, and it would have taken quite some time to translate and legibly transcribe Goliath's records for a layperson's ease. She had gone to enough trouble as it was just sorting through Goliath's prodigious records to weed out the information Maddie had asked for, so Maddie couldn't be upset at this minor stumbling block. She did worry that she would have to wait for Nadia to make sense of the information but the Internet came to her rescue. Soon enough she was reading Goliath's chart like a pro—an inept, poorly-trained, mind-numbingly slow pro.

Nadia hadn't exaggerated about Howard's tendency to seek medical attention for Goliath. No wonder he was so comfortable at the vet's office—he'd spent half his life there. If the information before her represented just a small portion of Goliath's medical history, then Nadia's office must be his home away from home. Maddie couldn't believe the wealth of information she had on Goliath even after Nadia had weeded out everything other than what she'd asked for. After seven pages of notes on Howard's overreaction to even the slightest fluctuation in Goliath's health, appearance or behavior, including a visit for an eye infection that Howard insisted Goliath had picked up from a Mastiff at the dog beach (rather than the filthy, stagnant water to be found at the dog beach), Maddie finally got to material that might be of use—if she could understand it.

Though there was nothing in the file about dog shows, Nadia had kept careful notes about Goliath's stud activities— ten pages' worth of meticulous records on his potential partners and the successful pairings. Unfortunately, all of the information Maddie really wanted had been written in a code for which the Internet did not provide a key. It looked like Nadia had recorded Goliath's transactions, so to speak, according to his mate's name, but then a series of letters and numbers followed each one. Each entry was followed by a date, but Maddie didn't know if that was an examination date, a breeding date or the date of some other significant event. There were at least fifteen entries with a similar set of letters and numbers, none of which made sense. Several sheets of paper were filled with coded information on dogs with high-minded names like Regina, Empress Josephine, Athena, Ophelia, Duchess, Princess, Portia and Bianca, some of the names circled or checked off, most with an X in the margin. She didn't know how to begin sorting through the information on her own, and she had no idea which information, if any, would lead her to Howard's killer.

Maddie could surmise the meanings of some of the markings, but it didn't make her feel any closer to finding the answers she thought would magically appear. For instance, it seemed likely that Goliath hadn't mated with the dogs whose names had an X beside them, but did that eliminate those owners as suspects or make them more likely candidates? Some pet parents could get overly defensive and protective of their dogs. What if an owner had become enraged when his or her dog wasn't deemed worthy of mating with Goliath? It didn't seem like the most obvious motive for murder, but, Maddie supposed, killers weren't generally known for their logic.

She could also guess that at least some of the letters by the dogs' names were the owners' initials, but which ones? And even if she guessed correctly on both counts, it would be nearly impossible to track someone down based on his or her initials, especially since she had no way of knowing where in the state—or the country, for that matter—that person might live. A frustrated sigh escaped her as she realized she was going to have to ask Nadia for help after all.

And then what? Call each owner and ask if perchance they'd murdered Howard after somehow learning that Goliath wasn't quite the purebred they'd been led to believe? It hardly seemed likely that the guilty party would confess, no matter how nicely she asked.

So she was back where she had started, except that now she felt disappointed and hopeless. She'd been so sure that the information she needed would be in Goliath's file, that Goliath's past was the key to Howard's death. She wasn't yet ready to give up that idea, but how would she figure out the truth? Her frustration mounting, she decided to set the befuddling files aside for the time being and take the boys for the walk they should have gotten before she plunged into her pointless quest to understand what had happened to Howard.

"I wish you could tell me what to look for," she said to Goliath as they strolled north, engulfed in the near-deafening crescendo of the cicadas' musical buzz. "I know the answer is there. I just need to figure out how to find it."

Though she'd embarked upon this walk to clear her mind, her thoughts never strayed far from Howard, Goliath and how their history could have led to murder. She knew that there was something in those files. There had to be. She couldn't explain her certainty about that any better than she could explain the connection between Goliath and Howard's death, but something she'd read in the file nagged at her mind, and she was determined to figure it out.

Following the boys as they headed east (probably with the off-limits beach in mind), she attempted to organize her chaotic thoughts by reviewing everything she'd learned from the beginning of her investigation. The familiar scenery of her neighborhood stretched out before her as her thoughts gradually succumbed to her need for order. One by one they fell in line until suddenly, like a fog lifting or a spotlight illuminating the one thing she'd been searching for, a reluctant memory stepped forward. Realization dawned, and though she had no way of proving it, she knew who had killed Howard.

Turning the boys to head back home, Maddie pulled out her cell phone and dialed Detective Fitzwilliam's number for what she hoped would be the last time. She was so busy bracing herself for his verbal onslaught that she was momentarily caught off-guard when the call went to voice mail. "Great time for a break, detective," she grumbled while she waited for Fitzwilliam's curt message to finish stating the obvious—that he wasn't available.

Once home she called Dottie to fill her in on her suspicions. "Are you sure, cupcake?"

"Not even remotely," she laughed, but in truth she'd never felt more certain about anything in her life. "Goliath and I are going to head over there to try to find some evidence while we wait for Detective Fitzwilliam to return my call."

"I know I've encouraged your detective work up to now, sweetbreads, but this is where I have to draw the line. You're talking about confronting a murderer—scratch that, a violent murderer."

"I'm not confronting anyone, Dottie. I'm just going to ask a couple of questions. Goliath will be with me. I'll be fine."

"Just in case, I'll call that odious detective again and try to get him to meet you there."

"Fine," Maddie agreed. "And I'll call you as soon as we're finished."

"See to it that you do, pumpkin."

CHAPTER TWENTY-EIGHT

Maddie was surprised by the modest aspect of the house that stood before her. From what she knew of its occupant, appearances—particularly if grandiose and pretentious—were everything. Maybe not everything, she corrected herself after considering how much trouble Howard had gotten himself into with that line of thinking. She had no plans to follow his lead.

Nevertheless, her surprise continued when the front door opened to reveal a dowdy middle-aged man in a red plaid button-up short-sleeve shirt and brown Sansabelt pants. He looked like a casually dressed, beardless Santa Claus on a moderately successful diet.

Apparently just as surprised to see Maddie, the man blinked uncomprehendingly several times before his eyes fell on Goliath and a giant smile stretched across his ruddy face. It was hardly the reception Maddie had expected. For his part, Goliath shifted nervously, unwilling or unable to settle down. He seemed simultaneously nervous and eager, a reaction she had anticipated, at least in part.

"Hello Goliath. Come to see the wife and kids?" the man asked jovially.

Taking advantage of that opening, which was far better than anything she'd managed to come up with, Maddie agreed and introduced herself.

"Donald Charles." He shook her outstretched hand. "It's nice to meet you, Miss Smithwick. Duchess and the puppies are in the back bedroom," he said as he led Maddie and a still nervous Goliath through the house.

She allowed herself the pleasure of interacting with Duchess and four of the most adorable puppies she'd ever laid eyes on before asking, "Is your wife at home?"

"She should be back any minute. You're welcome to wait for her." The living embodiment of the adage "opposites attract," he smiled again and invited Maddie to stay with the puppies or join him in the kitchen while he tended to dinner. "You're welcome to join us for dinner," he offered, again with more kindness than his wife could have summoned if her life depended on it.

Maddie barely had the chance to decline his offer before the front door opened. By her side, Goliath crouched low with his tail tucked under him. The hair on his back stood up, and he emitted a low growl. Although she knew the police would see things differently, this was all the proof she needed.

"It's okay, buddy," she whispered and hoped she was right.

"What are you doing here?" Ruth Charles barked, an echo of their first meeting.

"Maddie brought Goliath to see the family," Donald, oblivious to the tension in the room, answered.

"I was also hoping to talk to you, Mrs. Charles," Maddie said in her most innocent voice.

"Is that right?" Ruth said, her eyes narrowed to menacing slits. "Donald, we're going to need some privacy. Will you go out to the garden and gather some vegetables to go with dinner?"

"All right," he said as he turned off the flame under the cast iron skillet he'd been using to fry chicken. "I know how you ladies are when it comes to your girl talk. No men allowed," he joked before he kissed his wife's cheek and headed blithely out the door.

"What did you want to talk about?" Ruth's curiosity caught Maddie off guard. Did she really not know what Maddie was there for? Perhaps it would be safer to play it this way.

"I wanted to apologize." Maddie stroked Goliath's fur for reassurance. It didn't seem to help either of them. "I was rude to you when we met last week, and I'm sorry."

"Oh." Ruth was visibly confounded. Maddie wondered if it was the fact that she had apologized that threw her off (though she suspected that Ruth was accustomed to people apologizing, even groveling). More likely, she had expected something else from Maddie and was perplexed when she didn't get it. That wouldn't last long. "Apology accepted." Ruth clapped her hands together with an air of finality. "Thank you so much for stopping by." She fluttered her hands at Maddie, a gesture that suggested she would grab Maddie by the arm and escort her out, if not for the menacing dog by Maddie's side.

"Just one more thing." Aside from the curious lift along her eyebrows, Ruth remained perfectly still, waiting for whatever bomb Maddie was about to drop. "How did you know I was a dog walker?"

"Excuse me?"

"When we met, you knew I was a dog walker, but I didn't tell you."

"Someone else must have mentioned it to me."

"No. You arrived late, and I was the first person to speak to you." Ruth's face hardened, and Maddie felt a chill pass through her. In spite of the warning signals that Ruth, Goliath and her own body were sending her, she forged ahead. "I figure you must have seen me walking a dog that you knew belonged to someone else."

"That's ridiculous," Ruth huffed. "I don't keep a mental catalogue of every dog in the city."

"But you obviously know Goliath, and I'm betting you saw me take him out last Tuesday morning. In fact, I think you waited until you saw me leave Howard's house with Goliath and then snuck in to kill Howard while he was alone."

Without warning Ruth crossed to the stove, grabbed the skillet in which Donald been preparing their dinner and swung it at Maddie's head. Instinctively, Maddie raised her arm in time to block Ruth's swing, but she merely cushioned the blow with her own fist, which ricocheted off her face. In addition to burns where hot oil had splattered her body, she could feel a black eye forming, and the immediate explosion of pain in her arm was too much to bear. She cried out in pain and brought her other arm up to cradle one of her many injuries, dropping Goliath's leash as she did.

In that second Goliath lunged toward Ruth, who had cocked her arm to take another swing. The pan clattered across the floor as Ruth landed with a thud. Goliath, keeping his front paws on Ruth's chest, pinned her to the floor and barked incessantly. It took Maddie a minute to hear voices over the din of Goliath's anger. One of them was Ruth screaming, "He sullied my bitch!" over and over. Maddie was certain that anyone within a two-mile radius could hear the racket coming from Ruth Charles' kitchen.

As Maddie struggled to remain conscious and upright, Ruth's kitchen filled with people. Donald, clutching an overflowing basket of tomatoes and leafy greens, rushed through the back door, mouth agape, and surveyed the chaos before him. At the same time, the police, led by Detective Fitzwilliam, had charged in the front door. Fitzwilliam, as stunned as Donald Charles, barked orders at the officers who surrounded him, including Officer Murphy, who pulled Goliath off the still struggling Ruth Charles before turning her attention to Maddie. Through all of the commotion, Maddie thought she heard Dottie chastising Ruth Charles for her reprehensible behavior, but since she could focus neither on Dottie's voice nor on the proximity of the gorgeous Officer Murphy, she suspected she might be delirious from pain.

CHAPTER TWENTY-NINE

As a girl, Maddie had secretly longed to have a broken bone. It wasn't really the injury she wanted but rather the sympathy and attention and a cast full of signatures to show that she was loved. She'd witnessed this incredible, affectionate phenomenon in second grade when her best friend Leila had broken her arm and been excused from homework for a month and instead had received a steady stream of visitors, stuffed animals, ice cream and cookies.

What Maddie hadn't witnessed was the aggravation, inconvenience and irritation of wearing a cast. She was ready to tear the thing off her arm after a day. She didn't know how she would last for four weeks, especially considering the second-degree burns she'd gotten from Ruth Charles' searing weapon of choice. Maddie also wasn't thrilled with the mental fog she'd been living in thanks to the pharmaceutical industry's most potent painkillers. The drawbacks to being broken far outweighed the perks, and Maddie found herself mentally apologizing for the petty jealousy of her seven-year-old self to any deity that would listen and deeply regretting ever making that ridiculous wish. While she was glad she hadn't let Ruth kill her, if she ever had to face a skillet-swinging maniac again, she might try ducking instead.

The day after Ruth's arrest—at least Maddie thought that's what day it was—both of her parents stayed with her all day long. Her mother cared for the dogs and prepared food for which Maddie had no appetite, her father installed her new windows, and they both monitored her as closely as they could without suffocating her.

Throughout the day, she received business updates from Patrick. After the fourth text—to let her know that Pam Withers, who had abruptly cancelled her initial consultation with Maddie and Patrick, was suddenly interested in their services again—he suggested that they might want to hire more walkers. Apparently Maddie had been on the news— "Local Dog Walker Captures Killer"—and now everyone wanted to hire her. It took some of the sting out of her ordeal, as did most of her other encounters with the outside world.

At some point she'd received an enormous bouquet of flowers from Adam, Albert and Alphonse with a signed dog walking contract attached. From that, Maddie assumed that Dottie had talked to them and that she was forgiven for ever suspecting them of murder.

By far, the least pleasant interaction of the day was Detective Fitzwilliam's forty-five-minute lecture on leaving police work to the police. He grudgingly filled her in on what she'd missed after she'd blacked out from pain: Ruth Charles had, in fact, committed a heinous murder because Goliath's parentage hadn't been up to snuff.

"How did she find out?" Maddie wasn't sure Fitzwilliam would answer her questions, but right now he was her only option for information.

"Shelly Monk spilled the beans," he offered. "Apparently Howard was blackmailing her, sort of."

"How does one 'sort of' blackmail a person, especially someone who has no money?"

"By agreeing not to press charges for assault in exchange for Shelly's continued silence about Goliath's past."

"So Shelly pushed Howard down the stairs? Dottie is going to love that."

"From what I can gather, Shelly wanted money that Howard wouldn't give her. He still refused, even after his spill down the stairs, so Shelly went to Ruth."

Stunned, but grateful to have answers, Maddie listened patiently as Fitzwilliam made some sense of the events of the last week and a half. She was relieved to learn that Ruth's husband had been clueless about Howard's deceit and the role his wife had played in his death, and that Donald had decided to retire Duchess from dog shows and breeding. He'd also found homes for all of the puppies, one of them being with Detective Fitzwilliam.

After that happy news, the censorious remainder of their one-sided conversation had been hard to endure. Maddie couldn't imagine how much worse it would have been if she'd been coherent for the whole thing. Even so, the most difficult encounter of the day had been with Nadia. With equal parts of sympathy and reproach, Nadia had looked at her with such pitying anger that Maddie almost wished Ruth had put her in a coma.

"You promised you would tell the police what you found."

"I tried. The detective didn't answer his phone." She shrugged as if to suggest that taking matters into her own hands, rather than leaving a message and waiting for Fitzwilliam to return her call, was her only recourse.

"So you decided to break your other promise to be careful?"

"I thought I was being careful." She shrugged again. "No one regrets this more than I do, believe me."

Nadia's posture fell. "I doubt that's true," she said. She sank onto the couch beside Maddie and grabbed her good hand. "I helped put all of this in motion. My actions, my choices led to Howard's death and your injuries."

Maddie opened her mouth to object, but Nadia stopped her. "I know that Ruth Charles and her unhealthy purebred obsession are directly responsible, but she wouldn't have been teetering so dangerously close to the edge if I hadn't helped Howard manipulate her. It's not much different from handing an arsonist a box of matches and a can of gasoline and hoping he uses his better judgment."

"Except that you didn't know Ruth was dangerous. You didn't mean to hurt anyone."

"No, but that doesn't make Howard any less dead, does it?"

Maddie shook her head. She felt nauseous, and she wasn't sure if it was from the medication, the conversation or her dread of what Nadia was going to say next.

"I need some time alone to deal with this, my part in it and what it all means." The tears in Nadia's eyes as she spoke matched those in Maddie's.

"You know, it's not very nice to break up with a girl who's loopy on painkillers." Maddie's attempt at humor fell flat, but still she tried to keep her tone light. "Not smart either. I might not remember we had this conversation." She smiled weakly, knowing that this moment, and the ache associated with it, would stand out for a long time to come.

"Just give me a little time," Nadia said and kissed Maddie's cheek. "Oh," she turned back as she was halfway out the door, "I'm getting a dog—Goliath's daughter. Her name is Mabel. Maybe you'll get to meet her someday soon."

"I'd like that." Maddie offered another feeble grin, glad that at least something good had come out of this mess.

Moments later Granny appeared on Maddie's doorstep.

"Jehovah's balls!" she gasped and almost dropped the plate of oatmeal cookies she'd brought to aid her granddaughter's recuperation. "You're more battered than all the foods at the county fair. I should have made a double batch."

Maddie nibbled at one of the cookies, though she had even less of an appetite than before, and amazingly she did feel a little better. She polished off two more magical cookies before Dottie swept majestically into the room awkwardly holding a large wrapped box. Anastasia, off leash but ever obedient, followed Dottie, then went to join her friends in the corner. All three dogs cuddled together, as if life couldn't have been more perfect than it was at that moment.

"I need you to watch Anastasia for a few days. I'm letting my possibly future ex-husband take me to Cancun for a test drive."

"No problem as long as she doesn't expect any long walks. I'm mildly incapacitated at the moment." She nodded in the direction of her cast, in case Dottie had forgotten about her injury.

"She'll have a blast roughing it with the boys," Dottie said and grinned. "Now, open this, pumpkin. It will make everything better."

Maddie glared at her friend for a moment, wondering if she had to issue another reminder that she was living life one-handed at the moment.

"Let me help you with that," Granny offered before removing the paper and opening the box to reveal an acoustic guitar.

"You got me a guitar?" Dottie beamed expectantly at her. "As get well presents go, it's fairly unconventional, especially since I don't know how to play the guitar."

"That's what makes it perfect, muffin. Once you're liberated from your cast, you can learn to play. Think of it like physical therapy." Maybe it was the latent effects of the painkillers, but Dottie's logic actually made sense to Maddie. "And once you learn a couple of Indigo Girls songs, your bed will never be empty again."

"Gee, thanks." Maddie refrained from rolling her eyes. She wasn't going to open any doors to a discussion of her love life, so she quickly changed the topic. "Who was your trainer? Goliath needs some obedience lessons."

"So you can more easily find him a good home?"

"No," Maddie answered, looking at the dogs sleeping on her living room floor. All of them, even Anastasia, were part of her pack. "So he can stay here," she said and smiled.

Bella Books, Inc.

Women. Books. Even Better Together.

P.O. Box 10543
Tallahassee, FL 32302

Phone: 800-729-4992
www.bellabooks.com